BETA TROOPS

LEIF J. ERICKSON

Table of Content

Introduction

The first lesson that any person wishing to work for the government should learn is that any government can be brought down. It doesn't matter how powerful the military, how wealthy the government is, how righteous or evil they are, or how controlling they are, any government can be brought down if the will of the people is strong enough to overcome the determination of the government.

The United States of America stood as a beacon of freedom and wealth for almost 250 years before the civil wars started. No one was absolutely sure how they started. It could have been the massive division between the two parties, the overwhelming debt, the nation building military, or the apathy of the people in electing their government officials, but the civil war started and when the dust settled, America looked very different than before.

The acronym U.S.A. was still sometimes used, however the initials now stood for the Unified States of Alpha, which was a joke to those who hated the government of U-Cam, or the Unified Can Am Mex government. U-Cam was a collection of over ninety percent of the old U.S.A., fifty percent of Mexico, and twenty percent of Canada. The civil wars that gripped America were so destructive that they spilled over into its neighboring countries, taking parts of them down with them.

During the final fleeting days of the sixty year war, a losing faction decided that they were going to try a desperate gambit to attempt to turn the tide of the war back to their favor. In their attempt to seize control of the government, the Freedom Explorers, as they were known, released the monstrous Shackle Virus. The Shackle Virus attacked protein manufacturing centers of the body, creating a situation where humans cannot manufacture needed amino acids within the body and to survive must be fed a synthesized amino acid, once a week, to avoid a slow and painful death.

The Freedom Explorers had the needed amino acid compounds ready to use but before the Shackle Virus took effect, the Alpha Troops, led by the Ross family, wiped the Freedom Explorers out, along with the two other groups that were vying for control of the country. The Ross family found the synthesized compounds and began to develop more and more to keep everyone in the country alive. The first years of the Ross Empire saw a rebirth of the country. After so many years of war the people were ready for peace and the first Emperor Ross made sure there was peace throughout the country.

It didn't take many years to discover that Emperor Ross wasn't exactly what he'd claimed that he was going to be. He ruled with an iron fist. His promise to hold elections for a senate and state governments kept getting pushed back. Political dissenters disappeared in the night. The true nature of the emperor was revealed when a small uprising occurred, the people wanting representation, and Emperor Ross withheld the compounds and allowed the group to die. He said that any group or person who spoke out against them, tried to stand against them, or who worked against him would die.

A scientific arms race quickly began to develop the compounds so the people wouldn't be reliant on the government. Scientists quickly discovered that the compounds were so complex that they couldn't unlock the secrets of the compound. When the emperor discovered that they were working on unlocking the compound he withheld the compound and let the scientists die.

When the people reached a fever pitch over all the evils of Emperor Ross and wanted him gone, he allowed the election of a Prime Minister. The Prime Minister was to listen to the people and bring their pleas to the Emperor but he was only a stooge, he did the Emperor's bidding. Nothing changed.

The people started to long for the days of war, when the government didn't pay attention to their lives. A bright light came when Emperor Ross's daughter killed her father in the night and took the mantel of Empress Ross. She didn't rule like her father, she allowed the Prime Minister to dominate the country while she entertained herself with parties and a never-ending supply of men to keep her occupied.

Like her father, Empress Ross met her ultimate end at the hands of one of her children. The only son that she claimed killed his mother, strangling her in her sleep, when he was only fourteen years old. He assumed the title Emperor Ross II, held elections for a new Prime Minister, and started ruling the country like his predecessors. Emperor Ross II took the terror to a new level when he began to utilize the Alpha Troops to their fullest extent.

The Alpha Troops are genetically engineered warriors created by scientists who worked for the Ross family before they became rulers. The troops are stronger, smarter, faster, and totally loyal to the Ross Empire. The troops start training at a young age, learn multiple weapons and fighting styles, and thanks to the genetic engineering, develop genius intelligence. Their loyalty is assured in two different ways. First, it's breed into them with the engineering. Second, if any ever tried to defect, they wouldn't receive the needed amino acids to keep them alive.

Emperor Ross II, now in his twentieth year of rule, has maintained peace within the country by scaring the population into submission. His children are kept away from him to avoid a changing of the guard by a knife. His Prime Minister, Garret Boyd, takes a pleasure in watching citizens suffer.

No longer the beacon for peace and freedom, the old United States turned into a cesspool of crime, drugs, gambling, prostitution, and death. The police, run by the Alpha Troops, redefine corruption. The government uses taxes to make sure no group or family can gain the wealth to challenge them. The fear that Emperor Ross will pull the compounds and allow people to die is an ever-present threat.

However, hope is never far away when people still believe that hope is possible. There will always be people who remind us that the government is here to serve the people, the people are not here to serve the government...

Chapter #1

The water calmly broke against the side of the massive red freighter barge as rough seamen quickly scurried about, tying ropes and lowering gangplanks. The equipment came to life as the lights turned on and the sounds of industry filled the air and overtook the sounds of the soft but powerful ocean. The docks had been calm until the ship berthed at pier 14 on the foggy, warm night. As the men rushed about, a pair of black semis slowly drove down the pier with their flatbed trailers ready to receive the payload off the ship and move it instantly.

As the seamen worked to get the barge ready to unload, they couldn't help but notice a few men dressed all in black who carried large black automatic rifles board the ship and take position to protect whatever precious cargo the ship had carried. They worked quicker with the men there, knowing whenever extreme protection was needed, trouble would most likely follow. The ship's manifest indicated a pair of cargo containers listed as having been shipped under the highest priority although they would go to a small, local barber shop.

Carl Buss, the pier foreman, watched the bustle as the men shuffled the cargo cartons around to find the pair of containers the semis would pick up. Carl understood those situations. He didn't ask what was in the shipping containers, nor did he care. He simply wanted to get them off his docks as quick as possible. As Carl watched, the trucks stopped next to the ships in the loading area and a man exited the passenger seat of the front semi and approached him.

"You the foreman?" the man barked.

Carl studied the man. He was big, with short black hair and a black beard. Carl couldn't tell how much of the man's impressive bulk was real and what was from the long black trench coat he wore. He didn't know how the man functioned on a hot night in such a heavy jacket. The man walked right up to Carl and stood a pace too close for comfort.

"I said," the man barked again. "Are you the foreman?"

"Yes I am," Carl said quickly. "How can I help you?"

"Have you secured the area?" the man asked. "We have to know the area is secure before we begin to transfer those containers to the trucks."

"It is secure," Carl said. "We have multiple security devices in place. There's nothing to worry about here."

"The hell there ain't," the man said.

"And you are?" Carl asked.

"Devon Marks," Devon said quickly. "I'm in charge of this cargo. We need to move it quickly. The cargo itself is...sensitive."

"We have our schedule," Carl said. "It will be unloaded promptly. They are moving the upper crane over right now."

Carl and Devon looked down the docks and saw a crane slowly moving toward them. Devon looked at his watch and then back to the crane. His manner was impatient and rushed. Carl never could figure out why they always got so agitated while they moved cargo at night. Carl shook his head and looked back at his working men; he was proud of the good job they had done.

"You've scanned the entire docks?" Devon asked. "Made sure there were no Alpha Troops here?"

"Why would Alpha Troops be here?" Carl asked.

"I don't want to be held up by inspections," Devon said handing Carl a thick envelope. Carl looked inside and saw thousands of dollars, the same as when any of the ships carry cargo for small companies that have no reason to be receiving cargo crates. "We need to be out of here soon."

"Of course sir," Carl said.

"Who the hell is that?" Devon asked pointing down the docks.

Carl picked up his binoculars and looked out at the two shadows moving down the docks. Carl saw two stunning women, both tall and lanky, with well-defined curves and shapely bodies. They both had long curly hair, one fire red the other blonde. The women each wore an abundance of makeup. The redhead was wearing a leather miniskirt with a barely there leather top, both black with tall black boots. The other woman wore a shiny, tight, strapless silver dress with a very short hem and matching heels. Carl chuckled as he watched the women seductively walk toward the boat.

"I asked you a goddamn question," Devon said. "Who the hell are they?"

"Water rats," Carl said. "A pair of hookers. Look pretty hot though, I'm sure they are higher priced girls, not the cheap tramps who normally hang around the docks."

"Have you seen them before?" Devon asked.

"I don't associated with those types," Carl said. "We don't need to report them but that doesn't mean I'm going to hire them."

"The men do?" Devon asked.

"Often," Carl said. "The girls know these boats have been on the water for months and these men receive their final pay and trip bonuses before getting off. They have plenty of money for booze and women."

"I don't like it," Devon said as he pulled out a communicator and spoke into it. "Green leader, two inbound from west dock. Apprehend and detain until we have left the perimeter."

"Copy," Green leader's voice came through the communicator. "Orders received and understood."

"You think that's necessary?" Carl asked.

"I do," Devon said. "I think it's very necessary."

The men watched as more hustle and bustle took place on the boat and the women got closer to the loading area. A man approached the women as they walked. Carl noticed Devon had a smile across his face for the first time since he'd stepped out of the semi.

The women watched as a man dressed all in military black gear with a large handgun approached them. The women smiled, knowing this would be their first customer of the night. When the man got within four paces of the women he stopped and pointed his gun at them. The two women stopped and smiled, but didn't raise their hands.

"Stop where you are," green leader said. "Hands up."

"What's your name?" The redhead asked.

"Lance," Lance said. "I have orders to detain you. This is a private dock."

"That's real good Lance," the blonde said as she seductively moved her body while she stood in place. "Because we want to have a private party with you."

"A party with me?" Lance said.

"Anything you want Lance," the redhead said as she ran her hand over her body. "Anything you want."

"I do need to watch you," Lance said. "Move, this way."

Lance held the women at gunpoint as he made them walk along the dock. Lance looked up to where Devon was standing and flashed him a hand sign signaling all was well. Lance took the women into a side room and locked the door. The room was basic, white walls and floor, a folding table with chairs set in the middle. A partially played game of cards was spread about the table. The smell of cigars and cheap booze filled the room.

Lance turned and looked at the girls. He guessed they were each about twenty years old and knew they weren't ordinary cheap hookers. From the way they walked, the way they smiled, and the way they stood, Lance knew the women had been through the seduction schools that had become the norm in U-Cam. They were professional by every definition of the word. They surely knew every method there was to please a man. Lance smiled at the prospects of what was about to happen.

"So ladies," Lance said. "I'm the leader of this team. We were hired to protect some valuable cargo and I received a large hazard pay before I arrived. I'm supposed to keep you here and detained. So how much will it cost me for the two of you to keep me detained?"

"Both of us at once?" the blonde said. "We like that. Come to me Lance."

Lance slowly walked towards the blonde girl. He trembled because he was so excited, his mind racing with all the things he could do with these two ladies. Lance tried everything to calm himself; tried breathing slow and deep, tried focusing his attention elsewhere, but he was so aroused Lance couldn't even think straight as he placed his gun on the table and took the blonde woman's hand.

"What's your name?" Lance asked.

"I'm Crystal Dakota," the blonde said. "But I go by Dakota. This is my partner Tanna North."

"Those are beautiful names," Lance said. "Ladies, I've never done anything like this before."

"Sure you haven't," Dakota said. "Just relax and let us do the work."

Dakota kissed Lance twice before moving behind him. Tanna seductively danced while Dakota ran her hands over Lance's stomach and chest, his skin tingling with pleasure, arousal, wherever she laid her hands. Lance's eyes were glued on Tanna as Dakota moved her hands to Lance's head. Before Lance realized what was going on, Dakota tightened her grip on Lance's head and quickly twisted with great force which snapped his neck and killed him instantly. Lance fell to the ground as Tanna took his gun and pointed at him.

"He's dead," Dakota said checking for a pulse. "We don't have much time."

"Get his keys," Tanna said. "Check him for more weapons."

Dakota quickly searched over Lance's body. She grabbed his keys, his key cards, and an even smaller pistol and a black handled buck knife he carried in his boots. Dakota pushed her flowing blonde hair out of her face and looked out the small window to make sure no one was looking in the small room.

"We're clear," Dakota said. "We need to let them load the containers on the semis before we take them. They have too many armed guards watching..."

"Green leader," Devon's voice rang out in the room through his communicator interrupting Dakota's thoughts. "Status update."

Dakota and Tanna froze. They looked at the body and saw the communicator on his belt. Neither wanted to speak into it but they knew people would be looking for Lance and themselves very soon.

"Green leader status update," Devon's voice barked through the static communicator.

"We have to get out of here," Dakota said. "I'm sure they saw what building he took us in. They cannot find us here."

"Let's move out," Tanna said.

Dakota opened the back door and looked out making sure no one was watching. They quickly rushed along in the shadows, careful to avoid any people. They needed to get into a new position that would allow them to stop the trucks before they left the docks. The girls rushed around a corner and saw two armed guards blocking the way.

Tanna quickly raised Lance's gun and took two shots. She hit both men perfectly in their exposed necks. The men fell to the ground, never aware the two women had entered the hallway. Dakota rushed up to them and collected their rifles, knives, and keys. They quickly rushed further down the hall and into a small side room with a small round window that looked out over the dock.

Dakota looked out through the window and saw the guards in a panic. There were guards exiting the shack where they'd left Lance's body. People shouted and ran all over the docks. The crane was almost to the boat and it appeared the two containers were in position to be transferred.

"They know," Dakota said.

"Not good," Tanna said as she looked over the rest of the room.

The room was large with a long dark table surrounded by black chairs. One of the walls had a video screen and writing boards scribbled with ship arrival times and logistics. There was a large black metal desk on the other side. Only two small windows on the sidewalls. There was a control panel near the only door but the girls left the lights off. Tanna moved next to Dakota and peered out the window.

"What's the play?" Tanna asked

"We post here until they start loading the containers," Dakota said. "Then we move into position to take the trucks. I count at least fifteen more guards with guns."

"Sixteen," Tanna said. "One is hiding on top of the crane."

"These windows open?" Dakota asked looking over the window. "I have a plan."

"You shoot him from here and our position will be exposed," Tanna said."I know," Dakota said as she opened the window and pulled up a rifle she stole off the guards. "We'll have to move quickly. Once I fire we move to the ground floor. We cannot get into a shoot-out here. They have the position and the numbers."

"Divide?" Tanna asked.

"Our only chance," Dakota said.

Dakota adjusted the viewfinder on the scope of the rifle. The guard had filled the finder. Dakota saw a woman standing on the top of the crane, holding a massive rifle that was mounted but able to pivot in any direction. The woman's dark hair barely peeked out of her protective headgear. Dakota saw the woman wore only a long-sleeved, long legged black bodysuit, but was unable to determine if the garment was smart materials capable of deflecting a bullet. She knew a shot to the head wouldn't do anything because the headgear was bulletproof. Dakota wagered the bodysuit would be protective as well.

Dakota honed in on a very small patch of exposed skin, the woman's neck. The top went part-way up the neck and the helmet almost touched it, but there was a half inch of exposed skin. Dakota knew the little patch of skin would be the only place she could kill the woman. Dakota took a deep breath, held it, and squeezed the trigger.

Blood gushed from the side of the woman's neck as she collapsed. Dakota's heart skipped a beat. With all the noise of the docks she thought the gunshot would blend in but the woman fell from the top of the crane to the deck of the boat, which revealed to everyone that they were under attack. The workers on the dock quickly looked around to determine where the shot had come from.

Dakota quickly took two more shots, taking out two men who she thought looked to be barking orders. Dakota looked over the top of the boat and equipment and saw Devon and Carl standing on an operating platform. Devon was yelling into a communicator while Carl was watching all the insanity of what was going on. Dakota pulled the trigger, shooting Devon while leaving Carl alone.

Dakota rushed from her position and followed Tanna out of the room. They rushed down a flight of metal stairs and ran into a guard. The guard tried to pull his gun up but Tanna landed a punch and kick on the man. He took a step backwards, dropping his gun. Tanna tried to rush in on him but he took her to the ground, exactly as she'd planned. As the man struggled to punch Tanna, Dakota pulled a knife and slit his throat.

The girls quickly grabbed his weapons and rushed out of the backside of the building. As they moved along the edge of the building, gunshots rang out above them and bullets hit near them. They quickly ducked for cover as they looked up, trying to figure out where the shots came from. As they hid behind cargo boxes they watched three guards rush by. Once they passed, Dakota wanted to fire on them but couldn't because it would fully expose where they'd hidden.

Tanna realized there was a vent grate behind them. She popped the grate off and the girls snuck into the building they had run against. The small vent system was just large enough for the girls to wiggle their way through. They moved along until they got to a small storage room. They kicked the grate off and went into the room.

The room was full of random boxes placed in six different rows. There were shelving units on the walls with more boxes. The girls quickly made their way to the only door in the room. They waited for a moment before opening the door. Tanna opened it while Dakota hid behind on the opposite side. As the door opened, three more guards rushed in, weapons firing into the darkness of the room. Dakota and Tanna used kicks to break the guard's knees before snapping their necks.

"We can't leave them with weapons," Tanna said.

"We can't carry any more," Dakota said. "Quick, remove the firing pins."

The girls quickly field stripped the guns and removed the firing pins. Dakota then moved back from the open door with her rifle. By waiting only a moment she was able to kill two more guards. Dakota motioned to move out and Tanna fell in line behind her. They rushed along the exterior of the building. Dakota noticed the cargo boxes were loaded on the semis and the workers had secured the boxes on the trailers.

"Damn it," Dakota whispered to Tanna. "They are almost ready to go. We need to get into position or we're not going to be able to stop them. Quickly now."

Dakota quickly rushed into the open, running down a straight stretch of the docks. Tanna followed. They were almost to the end when gunshots rang out. The girls heard bullets flying over their heads. Dakota smiled, knowing they were so fast no sniper could have pulled them into the sights, and random firing with automatic weapons couldn't keep up with them either. The girls rushed into a small building and quickly closed the door.

When the door was closed the lights in the building came on. The building was a small equipment storage shed. There was no equipment in the middle of the shed but the walls had been lined with chains, binders, and other tools for securing cargo. Six guards stood in the middle of the shed with large black assault rifles aimed directly at Dakota and Tanna.

"Drop all your weapons," the leader barked. "Hands in the air. We know you are Alpha Troops."

"If you knew we were Alpha Troops," Dakota said as she obeyed his orders. "You'd know you cannot defeat us."

"There are six of us," the guard said laughing. "Armed to the teeth against two unarmed girls."

"Go get yourself a few more people," Tanna said with a smile. "Then it will be even."

"Arrogant fools," the guard said. "You are swine."

"We're not the ones breaking the law," Tanna said. "What are you smuggling here tonight?"

"If you only knew," the guard said, moving in on the girls. "You are blinded by arrogance."

The guards moved in on the girls. When they got close enough, Dakota and Tanna swung into action. Dakota grabbed the barrel of the guard's gun and pulled it past her and aimed it into one a guard's chest. Tanna pulled the trigger before kicking the guard in the knee so hard his knee exploded. He fell to the ground in excruciating pain and Dakota took the gun from his hands so blindingly fast the two guards hadn't even realized what she had done.

Tanna threw punches at the two guards left standing. Before the second man Dakota shot hit the ground Tanna had killed both of the other guards. The only guard left alive was the one they had on the ground. He was in the process of taking his helmet off. Dakota aimed the gun at his face.

"What are you transporting tonight," Dakota asked. "What?"

"Drugs, the guard said. "The most potent sweet leaf from the orient. What else would we be transporting? Millions of dollars' worth and they would have been on the streets before the sun rose this morning."

"Trying to undermine our beloved Emperor Ross II?" Tanna said. "You deserve to die."

The guard simply laughed.

"What's so funny?" Dakota yelled.

"Yes," the guard said. "Drugs are illegal by order of the emperor. So tell me why he sold us these drugs and now, after we've paid for them, he's having his goon squad confiscate them?"

"You lie," Dakota shouted. "He would never do that."

"Oh yes he would," the guard said. "The greedy bastard's going to resell them. How do you think he pays for all his pleasures? This is the government's side business."

"Go to hell you lying sack of shit," Dakota said as she unloaded the gun in the man's face.

"We need to get going," Tanna said. "They'll be on the move."

Dakota grabbed a loaded gun off one of the dead guards and rushed out the door. The semis lumbered away from the dock area, black smoke spewing from their stacks. Guards hung off the sides of both trucks, holding weapons at the ready. The trucks drove fast, not slowing for turns and curves.

Dakota and Tanna checked the clips in their assault rifles as they got into position, confident they could bring the trucks to a stop. When the trucks were close enough, they opened fire which quickly removed the guards off the sides of the truck and blasted out the windows as they shot the truck drivers.

Both trucks crashed into buildings along the docks, showering the area in sparks, starting fires, and causing a small explosion, killing the remaining guards on the trucks they hadn't shot. When they were confident all the guards were dead, Dakota pulled out her communicator and called the rest of her team to clean up and take the confiscated goods in for processing. Dakota and Tanna looked over their work, proud of another job well done.

Chapter #2

The medical campus was an architectural wonder set on a hill of land within a cold, uninviting city known as Falling Ridge. It had formally been known as Washington D.C. The old city had been completely leveled during the wars but the first thing Empress Ross did was build a city of her own design and move the government back from New York where the first Emperor Ross had dictated. Where the White House once stood was a mega-castle and there were theaters and sporting arenas where the senate used to meet. Falling Ridge had become a culture center but under the rule of Emperor Ross II it had become a smut town. Drugs, gambling, and prostitution ruled the streets. What was once a grand city people from all over the world flocked to had become a dank and dirty afterthought, just like the city.

The only building that still looked fresh and clean was the medical campus which was the sole crown jewel of the town. It was in the Ridge Medical Facility where the Alpha Troops were genetically engineered. The Ridge Medical Facility had unlimited funding and free reign to get results by any means necessary and they used those rights to their fullest extent.

A doctor left the campus as the sun set on the city of depravity. He drove a basic car, a rusted, ten year old red Ford although he could have afforded something much nicer. He didn't wear a watch or any jewelry although he owned many gold pieces. The only thing he carried on him was a pistol. His car had been updated with bullet-proof plates on the sides and glass. The man was Doctor Chas Kent. Doctor Kent was an assistant researcher on the newest form of Alpha Troops, the Beta Troops.

Doctor Kent drove fast through the poor streets of Falling Ridge and tried his hardest to get to the interstate that would take him to his home in the suburbs as quick as possible. As Doctor Kent drove through the streets he saw Alpha Troops on patrol as they watched for anyone that may pose a threat to the government, in a word, they watched everyone. When Doctor Kent reached a red light and had to stop, he looked both ways and quickly sped through the intersection, not wanting to bring his car to a full stop with the people on either side of the streets.

Doctor Kent made it to the small suburb of Red Brook, a sleepy little town outside the megalopolis of Falling Ridge. Many of the higher level doctors who worked at The Ridge lived in Red Brook and paid for private security to patrol the streets and keep the crime out of the city. Doctor Kent turned into his apartment complex, parked his car, and took off running as he realized he was late to his appointment.

Doctor Kent ran down the sidewalks along the city streets. He continuously looked over his shoulders to make sure no one followed. He cut through a number of yards and buildings. Doctor Kent made sure the hire patrols didn't see him. He knew he couldn't miss the appointment. Not with the new information he had. Doctor Kent, like most of the citizens of U-Cam, hated the Ross family and their empire and was willing to do whatever it took to take them down.

Doctor Kent rushed into a small office building, down two flights of stairs and into a room guarded by a metal door. In the room was a small round table where three people sat. In one chair was Doctor Monte Prowl; a dignified and very proud man. He was tall and lank with slicked back black hair with subtle gray strands spread about. He had wide set green eyes with a prominent nose that dominated his face. His face had sharp angles and Doctor Prowl always looked like he was contemplating something. He wore a three piece gray suit with a black dress shirt.

Beside Doctor Prowl was Adam Plains, a stringy man with dull eyes and a shaved head. Adam sat in an open position with his thin arms down, and a droopy black mustache nearly covered his lips. He was muscular and did everything he could to keep himself that way. Adam had been on his way to becoming a doctor at The Ridge before he failed his classes. Adam had a brilliant mind but had lost himself into the pitfalls of Falling Ridge. Rather than study, he wasted his time in the gambling dens and spent his money on the games, drinks, drugs and women. After he rid himself of his addictions he had been discovered by Doctors Kent and Prowl.

Near the far wall sat a beautiful woman of only twenty-two years old; Jerrica Prowl, Monte's half-sister from a different mother. Jerrica was petite, only five foot tall with all around small features. Jerrica's eyes were set close together and surrounded by bright blue eye shadow around a small nose. Her narrow lips had been painted ruby red and sparkled when the light hit them. Her shoulder length straight brown hair contained streaks of blonde and she wore black slacks with a red blouse.

As beautiful as Jerrica was, Monte had to be very careful to make sure she was never kidnapped and forced to work in the pleasure houses he had already saved her from twice. Monte had been more of a father to her than their real father had been to either of them. Monte and Doctor Kent had secretly trained Jerrica in science to make sure she would be able to work with them on their project.

"I just received the report we've been dreading," Doctor Kent said as he entered the room. "They worked perfectly."

"They?" Doctor Prowl asked. "There was more than one?"

"Yes, two," Doctor Kent said as he sat down and tried to catch his breath from the run. "The initial report was no one expected them to be military."

"You're talking about the Beta Troops, correct?" Jerrica asked in her soft voice.

"Correct Jerrica," Doctor Kent said. "Two women everyone thought were nothing but street walkers killed most of the highly trained and heavily armed guards that had an experienced combat captain to guide them. It happened last night at the docks."

"What were they doing there?" Adam asked.

"A drug shipment came in," Doctor Kent said. "They had paid Emperor Ross II for the shipment; the Emperor confiscated it and had everyone who knew about it killed."

"Back to the Beta Troops," Adam said. "Killers that looked like hookers? It's not possible."

"It is possible," Doctor Kent said. "I saw the women myself. They looked like average people. The advantage we had with Alpha Troops was we knew who they were based on their size. Only Alpha Troopers would have arms and legs the size of tree-trunks. Even the women were abnormally large. It was the only way they got the strength they wanted. Now they get troops almost as strong with the required speed and skill but look like average people."

"Then we're done," Adam said. "There's no way we can combat that."

"Not so fast," Doctor Prowl said. "I'm betting there's a hook. What is it?"

"In working to create Beta Troops," Doctor Kent said with a smile. "I made a discovery."

"Relating to amino acids?" Jerrica asked hopeful.

"No," Doctor Kent said. "Relating to what gives the troops their strength, skill, speed, and intellect. I propose we create a compound that when injected into a trooper, would cause them to lose everything they've been given."

"Impossible," Adam gasped.

"Permanently?" Doctor Prowl asked. "Would they be destroyed for good?"

"The effects would not be permanent, no," Doctor Kent said. "I would estimate we would have at least an hour of time where they are back to their normal abilities."

"How does it work?" Doctor Prowl asked. "I didn't think we would be able to remove abilities without killing the subject."

"The genetic engineering they performed on them," Doctor Kent said. "Is permanent. To remove it completely we would have to kill them. What I discovered is when they are overloaded on a pair of amino acids, their blood slows and the body focuses on removing excess proteins. This has an interesting effect of slowing their muscles and their thinking. It takes about an hour for the body to remove the amino acids which allows them to function normally again."

"If you gave the pair to a normal person," Jerrica asked. "What would happen to them?"

"They would die," Doctor Kent said plainly. "Only the genetically engineered troops can handle it. Think about this though. We have the ability to neutralize the killers."

"For an hour," Adam said. "What good will that do us? What can we do with them for an hour?"

"More than you know," Doctor Kent said. "In that one hour window we can run tests. I have access to theory and data, nothing more. We can capture some Beta Troops and show Emperor Ross II we no longer fear him."

"The second we do that," Adam said. "He will find out who we are and withhold our amino acid supply. I thought that was our prime goal, figure out how to synthesize the amino acid so we don't need to rely on them."

"It is still our goal Adam," Doctor Prowl said. "This is a means to an end. I'm betting we can use one of the troops to reach our goal."

"We can develop a number of contingencies to work with," Doctor Kent said. "Our best plan would be to show the emperor we can take his troops out. Once we do that he will have no choice but to work with us on some level. We can then use the leverage we get to figure out the key to unlock the amino acids."

"He'll never work with us," Adam said. "He would rather the entire country die and start over than to bend to someone else's will."

"I agree with Adam," Jerrica said. "Emperor Ross II will never work with us. That said, I think we should use this to learn all we can about the troops. It might be a different story if we kill enough of them."

"Violence only begets violence sister," Doctor Prowl said.

"And violence is the only language a dictator understands brother," Jerrica said. "We have an opportunity here, one chance to right a wrong. How many people have suffered and died under the Ross Empire? How many people would be saved if the amino acid was freely available? The Freedom Explorers may have released the virus but there's no denying the Ross Empire has used it to their full advantage. It's time the people take back this country and give it the glory it once had."

"You're a dreamer," Adam said. "It would never work. Once they find out we are doing this we'll all be dead. It's been tried before."

"We have an obligation to humanity," Doctor Kent said. "If we have the chance to destroy evil we must take it or we are no better than the evil we are referring to."

"What should our play be then?" Jerrica asked. "We need to move swiftly. If they even suspect anything is going on we will be dead. We have to move like the whirlwind and strike before anyone even knows we're here."

"We must strike fear into Emperor Ross's black heart," Doctor Kent said. "Doctor Prowl can find out schedules for patrols. You must find when the new Beta Troops will be in the city. The amino acid pair can be placed on the tip of a dart, that's all it will take. We can take two Betas out and bring them to a secure place. We'll hold them until they agree to work with us in some capacity. While that's happening, we'll have another team kill a group of the Alpha Troops."

"There's never been a group of Alpha's killed before," Adam said. "It can't be done. They are so fast it's hard to hit them with bullets. Their systems can metabolize every known poison before they take effect. What are we going to do?"

"The plan will be simple enough," Doctor Kent said. "They will be hit with the darts and while they are down we'll shoot them."

"Many Alpha Troops have survived gunshots before," Adam said. "What makes you think this will be different?"

"Two in the heart," Doctor Kent said. "One in the head. I doubt they will be able to survive while they are still internally fighting the amino acid. The beauty of it is unlike poison, they have no resistance to the amino acid pair. It will take their systems by surprise."

"We know the Alpha Troops are watched by satellite," Doctor Prowl said. "How do we capture two and kill a group without being seen and followed?"

"There will be some tricks used," Doctor Kent said. "I remember reading about one that was used in the final throws of the first stage of the war. They needed to transport people without satellites seeing them. They used multiple vehicles and scrambled into rush hour traffic. There was no way to keep up with them all at the same time. They went through different tunnels and exited the vehicles they started in and moved to random vehicles like delivery trucks and school buses. We'll have to make the switch fast enough so there aren't other security troops on us."

"That could work," Jerrica said. "I have a backup plan if needed. Once we have them though, where are we going to take them?"

"We'll have to rent a place," Doctor Kent said. "Somewhere obscure and away from Falling Ridge. The outer suburbs would work best. I can get us enough fake credentials so no one will question it. We'll have to move fast though. Above all else, we cannot get caught with the troops. The public doesn't know about the Beta Troops and you can be sure the emperor won't parade them out on the airwaves and show them to the world."

"How soon do we want to move?" Jerrica asked.

"As soon as possible," Doctor Kent said. "Doctor Prowl, how soon do you think you can get the patrol schedules?"

"I'll have them tomorrow," Doctor Prowl said. "I'll have next week's schedule tomorrow which will give us enough time to rent a place and put together the final details of the plan."

"I just want to go on record," Adam said. "That I don't think this will work."

"Fine," Doctor Kent said. "But we are moving ahead with it anyway. By this time next week Emperor Ross II will finally know and understand fear."

Chapter #3

The mega-castle towered over everything else in the city because the emperor had passed a law ordering nothing in the city be built taller than his pleasure palace. She went as far as to cut down trees that were near the same height. Nothing was too expensive for the castle, nor was anything too large. Two hundred thousand square feet, five towers, two at each end and one in the center, stretched over one hundred and fifty feet into the air, casting their shadows over the two hundred foot long, five story castle.

The castle took five years to complete and Empress Ross made sure that everything was exactly the way she wanted it. All the floors were the finest marble that was imported from all over the world. Each floor was a different color and each wing had a different shade of that color. Gold, silver and platinum were inset throughout the castle. The windows were stained glass and depicted the story of all the wars and how the Ross Family came to power.

The first floor contained massive ballrooms, theaters, a small sporting arena, and the grand dining room. The second floor had offices and meeting chambers where much of the country's business was conducted. The upper floors were residences and playrooms. Every ceiling was over twenty feet tall and every wall had some form of decorations covering the majority of it. The grand entrance beneath the middle tower had a ceiling sixty feet tall, arching from the tower with a mosaic of glass which allowed multi-colored light to illuminate the over life-sized statues of the entire Ross Family.

The grounds of the castle were just as impressive as the castle itself. Looking out from the south towers was a one hundred acre hedge maze. To the north was a large open air sports arena. The east and west contained huge flower gardens spared with exotic plants and trees. The empire had never released the total cost of how much the palace and grounds actually cost but most people estimated it to be well over a billion dollars, all at the taxpayers' expense. A show of power to remind them just who was in control.

In a second story office, decorated in an ancient Egyptian fashion, a heavy-set tall man had finished playing with two women. The women, both fully trained in all forms of pleasure and seduction, were dressed to match the décor of the room. They wore ancient Egyptian costumes and the man wore a silk flowing, flashy multicolored robe over a pair of silk black shorts. The women were both tall and thick and of Mediterranean decent with dark skin and long black hair. One in her late teens and the other in her earlier thirties; they were Emperor Ross II's favorite and private concubines. Although Emperor Ross II had many other girls, he used these two more than any other.

As the youngest of the pair fed Emperor Ross II grapes, the door to the office opened and a short and sinister man with black hair, a black pointed goatee and black sunglasses over his narrow set eyes walked in. He wore a satin suit of all black and his fingers were covered in gold rings. The man's face was predatory, narrow and thin. The man's body was solid muscle as he took amazing care of himself.

"Charlie!" the man shouted. "Put your toys away, we have work to do. You were supposed to meet me in the prime office."

"Calm yourself Garret," Emperor Ross II said. "You'll give yourself a headache. I was having fun with some ladies."

"OUT!" Garret shouted. "Out now."

The older woman quickly left the room. The younger was slower to leave. She walked up to Garret and ran her hand over his chest.

"Rough day Prime Minister Boyd?" the girl asked. "I could help you release some of those tensions."

The woman's hand dropped past Garret's stomach and worked its way toward his pants. Garret grabbed the woman's hand and quickly pulled a large, gold plated pistol out of his jacket. He pushed the barrel of the gun into the woman's lower jaw.

"Be a dear," Garret said in his deep, raspy voice. "And get the hell out of my sight."

The girl slowly left the room with a pouty look on her face while Garret held his pistol on her until she was clear of the room. Charlie Ross moved from his comfortable lounge chair he'd shared with the women to his desk. Before he sat down Charlie filled a goblet with wine.

"Why'd you send her away?" Charlie asked. "She's very good. You cannot believe what that girl can do."

"I don't touch gutter trash," Garret said as he methodically put his gun away. "I'm getting fed up with having to chase you down Charlie. There's matters of state to attend to."

"You're the Prime Minister," Charlie said sipping his wine. "You handle it. I have better things to do."

Garret looked over Charlie with disgust. Where a tough, fit man once stood, now sat a fat, lazy slob. Once he had the country securely under his control, he slowly let himself go, little by little. At first it was a pleasure girl once in a while, a hit of drugs and a glass of wine. It escalated until it was all the time; daily with the women and constant wine and brandy. Garret couldn't remember the last time Charlie wasn't buzzed off of sweet leaf, the drug of choice for anyone dignified. Before Garret could continue, Charlie pulled an ornate tin of ground sweet leaf out of his desk, took a small pinch, and sprinkled the white powder on his tongue. It took only a few seconds, but Charlie had a moment of full body shivers before he relaxed back in his chair, a glassed look coated his eyes.

"There's been another attack," Garret said. "A rebel group tried to take out a grouping of Alpha Troops. There were heavy civilian casualties."

"I don't care," Charlie whined. "The Alpha Troops cannot be defeated. Who cares if someone dies in the crossfire? As long as it's not one of my women I simply don't care Garret."

"Very soon," Garret said. "If you don't start caring, a group of civilians will be using your disembodied head as a soccer ball."

"I'm far too protected for that," Charlie said. "You're depressing me. Leave now."

"LISTEN TO ME!" Garret yelled and knocked the wine glass from Charlie's hand. "We've run this country longer than anyone in the last hundred years and we did that by having a unified front. You and I kept the people in line and made then cower, and there was peace. Now, attacks are happening all of the time. People are testing the limits of what they can do. They don't fear us anymore."

"Then kill a few of them," Charlie said pouring a new goblet of wine. "Detain some. I don't care what. I'm the Emperor. I shouldn't have to deal with this garbage. I want my girls back here."

"I need you though," Garret said.

"What do you need me for?" Charlie asked.

"Without you," Garret said starting to pace the room. "Your eldest daughter Alexis would be in line for the empire. She's savvy and tough. The people like her. Alexis says that she will have elections for a senate and let the people have representation. She will destroy the Alpha Troops and she will enter the vaults, find the formula for the amino acid, and make it public. All of our power will be destroyed and the military generals will follow her. Without you, I'll be on the run."

"My son," Charlie said. "George will defeat her. She could never stand against her older brother."

"Alexis is good Charlie," Garret said. "Far more devious than you could ever imagine. She sent him a gift many years ago, a beautiful woman to pleasure him. The woman had strict instructions to get him hooked on some very debilitating drugs. His mind's been destroyed. Alexis did the same to any of the other children that supported you or George. Now Elizabeth and James support her both publicly and privately. Your other twelve children are either dead or so burnt out on drugs they couldn't run a race, let alone a country."

"Kill her," Charlie said. "Do it now."

"She's far too protected," Garret said. "We must be patient with her. Her efforts get her nowhere, the people tire of getting killed for her and soon you will have an heir that will be worthy of the Ross Empire. Three of your women are expecting. We will make one of them the heir to carry the empire but we have other matters to attend to."

"I have the money and ability," Charlie said. "We should take some of my women and go into exile, live out our lives in peace and leave all this stress behind."

"I'll exile you," Garret yelled as he pulled his pistol and aimed it directly at Charlie's head. "We are in this for the long run which will be much longer if you put your toys away and get with the program."

"We wouldn't be in this mess," Charlie said as he stood up. "If you'd killed Alexis when I ordered you to. She was only fourteen and you couldn't get the job done."

"She would have been dead," Garret said putting his gun away. "If you'd have provided me with accurate information. Enough of this bickering, we have matters we need to attend to. These attacks. People know what will happen to them if they oppose you yet they still attempt to challenge your authority."

"We need a large attack," Charlie said. "Something that kills thousands of people. Blame it on rebels and we step in and save the day."

"We've used that system too many times," Garret said. "The last time we did that was four years ago and too many people saw through it. They know what we'll do to maintain peace. All we want to do is keep U-Cam peaceful and war free. I don't know why they defy us."

"We still maintain the amino acids," Charlie said. "They know there's only so far they can push before we cut them off. We can manage this."

"We still have a problem with that," Garret said. "The Freedom Explorers had the formula hidden at some of their bases. We found it at three bases but we never found their rumored fourth base. The formula could still be hidden out there somewhere and if another group discovers the secret, we'll be done. There will be nothing to stop the masses from marching on this palace and wiping us out."

"Then why haven't we found that base?" Charlie asked. "We must find it."

"We have plenty of people looking for it," Garret said. "It's only a matter of time. We know which cities they were in. I'm willing to bet the hidden base was near one of their main bases. We are searching out all underground ruins we can find."

"Find them," Charlie said. "If I must stay here I want to be secure. Kill my daughter as well...check that, kill all my living children whether they are well or not."

"Alexis is the only one that matters," Garret said. "And she's in hiding. We haven't had a good report on her location in years...There is good news though Charlie."

"Why do you address me by my first name?" Charlie asked. "Shouldn't you call me by a formal title?"

"I should," Garret said. "But when you turned most of the country over to me I decided to refer to you as I did when we were young and friends. You don't rule like you use to."

"I would like to be addressed by a formal title again," Charlie said.

"When you go back to ruling the way you did," Garret said. "I will address you formally. Now to the good news. The Beta Troops worked perfectly. We couldn't have asked for a better performance from them. No one knew. Everyone was taken by surprise. They destroyed the guards that were there, and two of them were Alpha Troops. The Beta Troops didn't suffer at all in killing a mass group of highly trained killers."

"Perfect," Charlie said. "They look like normal people?"

"The two girls we used," Garret said, "were dressed like hookers. No one questioned it. When they killed a crane guard, Devon believed that someone else was attacking. He didn't know it was them. Their bullets were precise. They killed efficiently with their bare hands. Full grown Alpha Troop men had died by the Beta Troops' hands. I've watched video of it. We had cameras everywhere and the action is outstanding. We have our newest weapon, our Beta Troops, and it's deadlier than anything we've ever had before. Our intelligence indicates that no one is aware of them yet."

"We need to use them then," Charlie said. "They can infiltrate enemy cells and bring them down from the inside."

"Very impressive," Garret said. "I was thinking the same thing."

"I just want to be safe and enjoy myself," Charlie said. "I just want to enjoy my life and not deal with this stress anymore."

"There's one more thing you need to do today before you return to your pleasures," Garret said. "You must meet with the Beta Troops. You will be amazed at them."

"Good," Charlie said. "I'd love to see them. Take me to them now."

"Follow me," Garret said as he escorted Charlie out of the room.

Chapter #4

The tall red brick building looked plain. Although it had been newly built, the building had been constructed to resemble buildings that were erected almost two hundred years prior. It was rectangular with straight walls and ninety degree angles. The roof was flat with climate conditioning equipment mounted on top. The sign above the main entrance simply said 'Gym and Fitness' but the truth was far greater than the simple sign led on. This building was the Alpha Troops main training center.

Inside the center, on the twentieth floor, in a private workout room, two women were in the throes of their morning workout. Dakota and Tanna had finished running five miles on the track and moved on to lifting weights. Alpha Troops had many spotters and assistants when working out, but Beta Troops only conditioned in team pairs in order to develop a stronger bond within the team.

Dakota started bench pressing 650 pounds while Tanna spotted. The pair knew they were different from the Alpha Troops but wanted to stand out as the top troops from any group. Dakota pushed the weights up faster and harder than normal because she was upset by what the drug runner had said to her the night before. She couldn't believe the country and Emperor Ross II would be involved with drugs and double-crossing people. She thought it must have been a mistake and they had lied to save themselves.

The girls were in a private room with just enough space for the three multi-function workout machines that sat against the walls, the free weight rack, and mats in the middle of the room for ground workouts. As Dakota finished her one hundred rep set, the door to the private gym opened and Emperor Ross II and Prime Minister Garret Boyd entered the room. Dakota saw guards posted outside the room. Dakota set the weight bar on its cradle and stood in line with Tanna at full attention and saluted the Emperor.

"Emperor Ross II," Dakota said. "It's an honor, sir. Sorry we're not in proper formal attire."

Charlie studied the two women. They were both incredibly fit, tan, and beautiful. They were wearing tight, purple sleeveless crop tops with black hot pants; both with the U-Cam seal sown into them. The first thoughts that ran through Charlie's mind were of the pleasures that he could have with those two. A quick glance to Prime Minister Boyd told him he need to conduct business. Charlie breathed a heavy sigh.

"At ease," Charlie said. "As you were. I wish to see your workout."

Dakota nodded and returned to the bench. She finished her set and Tanna got on the bench and started lifting.

"Impressive," Charlie said as he looked at the 650 pounds of weight on the bar. "A normal person could never handle that much. That must be five times the amount of what you each weigh."

"I weigh one hundred twenty five," Dakota said. "Tanna weighs one nineteen. We know the standard Alpha woman can lift over eight hundred and the men one thousand. We are pushing ourselves to reach those levels."

"No need," Charlie said. "You can handle anyone out there. We have greater needs for you than simple strength. You are the ultimate secret weapon. I'm sure there's much you can do for your country."

"We're honored to serve you sir," Dakota said.

"Please," Charlie said with a smile. "Call me Charlie. There's not very many people I allow to be familiar with me, but you two, I would love to be very familiar with."

"Damn it Charlie," Garret said. "Knock it off. We didn't spend billions of dollars and decades of research for you to have more playmates. We're here for a reason ladies. We watched your performance last night."

"Hopefully," Tanna said as she got off the bench and spotted Dakota squat over one thousand pounds. "Our work was to your liking?"

"Beyond words," Charlie said. "You were perfect. No one had any idea that you two had done the killing. We have big plans for you."

"What do you mean?" Dakota asked.

"The Alpha Troops," Garret said. "Are noticeable. When men stand seven feet tall and have thirty-six inch biceps, women at six and a half feet with twenty-four inch biceps, it is very apparent that they are Alpha Troops. You two have the dimensions of regular humans yet you have almost as much strength as the Alphas and you have far more intelligence. We need to keep you silent long enough so we can smoke out a few traitor cells and kill them."

"We will kill anyone who stands against the empire," Dakota said.

"I know you will," Garret said. "There have been many recent attacks against the Alpha Troops. We are going to request you two seek out these cells of resistance, infiltrate them, and destroy all who are a part of them. You must discover all the members and leave none of them alive."

"Orders understood," Dakota said as she and Tanna switched positions. "Do you have any intelligence on where these groups meet or the best tactic for us to gain entry into their groups?"

"I have compiled a report," Garret said. "It will be in your quarters when you return. We have the names of a few people and a location they often frequent. You will be required to use stealth in obtaining this information. You must have the names of every member of the cell before you start killing them. We don't want any to run or figure out what you two are."

"There won't be any left when we are done sir," Dakota said. "I assure you of that."

"I've no doubt in your abilities," Charlie said gazing at Dakota. "You must have some amazing abilities. You must come to my chambers sometime. We have wonderful parties there. I'm sure you would fit right in and have a stunning time."

"It would be an honor to join you," Dakota said. "Anytime."

"Just focus on the task at hand ladies," Garret said as he glared at Charlie. "You can pleasure him later."

"I have one question for you," Dakota said. "It's something that's bothering me although I don't know if it's my place to ask."

"You can ask me anything," Charlie said.

"Okay," Dakota said taking a deep breath. "When we were killing the drug runners last night, one of them said that they had purchased the drugs from you, that you were confiscating them and were going to resell them. That's not true, is it?"

"Of course not," Charlie said with a smile.

"I knew he was lying," Dakota said cheerfully.

"We sold them the drugs," Charlie said. "Confiscated them and are going to use them at my parties. When foreign dignitaries arrive we must be sure to have plenty of party supplies for them. My personal supply also need to be kept full at all times. It is the way of the empire."

"I had no idea," Dakota said. "I thought drugs were illegal though."

"For the commoners," Charlie said. "Gives us a good reason to arrest those who stand against us. The average person has no idea what pressures we are under to govern and run an empire. It takes so much work and I need to have a way to relax, a way to keep myself level. All my administrators do. The drugs are just one privilege we have that they don't. You understand, don't you?"

"Yes," Dakota said. "You have nothing to worry about Emperor Ross II. We will find your rebels and kill them. There will be nothing left when we are finished with them."

"I've no doubt of that," Charlie said. "Good day."

Emperor Ross II and Prime Minister Boyd left the room while the girls continued to switch back and forth on the weight machines. Dakota seemed to be more aggressive than ever as she lifted massive amounts of weight over her head. Tanna couldn't figure out why Dakota was being so aggressive.

"What's wrong?" Tanna asked.

"Why does something have to be wrong?" Dakota asked.

"I know when you're mad," Tanna said. "We've trained together so much I can tell just by the look in your eyes that something's on your mind. Just spill it."

"What the Emperor is doing," Dakota said. "It's wrong."

"What's wrong?" Tanna asked.

"Selling drugs," Dakota said. "Then stealing them back. Those people we killed last night were only following orders given by the same people we were taking orders from."

"So?"

"So what happens," Dakota said. "When we end up on the other side of those orders?"

Tanna mouthed a silent 'Oh' as she thought about the implications of what Dakota had just said. They had always simply followed orders and not worried about any of the dealings of the empire. Their job was safety and security and that's all they really knew. Tanna knew what Dakota was implying as Dakota picked up a sixty pound dumbbell and moved to the mat on the middle of the floor. Dakota started using the weight in a core workout as Tanna looked on.

"What's our plan going to be then?" Tanna asked. "What do you think we should do?"

"We are going to look over the file," Dakota said. "And we are going to do our jobs the way Emperor Ross II wants us to do them. We must make sure we perform better than any other group in the core. We must outperform and outclass the entire Alpha Squad. That way, when looking at whose side we're on, there will be no questions."

"We should show the emperor how good we are," Tanna said. "We should challenge any Alpha pair to a combat and let the emperor watch. When he sees what we can do he'll surely make us his favorites. Then we would have nothing to worry about."

"That's a really good idea," Dakota said switching the weight to her other hand. "We could show him that we are better in every way than the old troops. We could even position ourselves to be the leaders to train the new Beta Troops as they come down the line. We must be prepared though. We can't just win, we must destroy them."

"That will be easy to do," Tanna said. "We'll need information first."

"What information?" Dakota asked.

"On everything about them," Tanna said. "I know exactly how to get what we need. We have training that the Alpha women don't have and I'm sure I can leverage that into finding out precisely what we need to do to beat them in combat."

"Alpha women received no seduction training," Dakota said. "And the men only spend time with women from the seduction schools. You sure you can pull it off?"

"Very," Tanna said. "Tonight I'll go to two of them and I'll blow their minds away. Once they are in an open and talkative state I will extract the information we need."

"Good," Dakota said as she finished her set.

The pair finished their workout in silence. After two hours of intense training the pair showered then returned to their private quarters for mental training. The Alpha Troops had schools that focused on their specific needs, but Beta Troops had been engineered to be intelligent enough to learn on their own. They had no need for coaches or teachers. It was a benefit to them in that there was no one to give away the secrets of how they had been trained.

Dakota and Tanna lived together in a small, two bedroom brick house on the outer edge of the palace grounds. Their house sat in a row with similar houses that were for the management of staff for the palace and palace campus grounds. Betas had been kept in two person teams where the Alpha Troops had their own massive barracks complex. The Beta's were spread out as well and no pairs of Beta teams lived near each other.

The interior of their house was as basic as could be. The kitchen was the fanciest room because the government at least had the knowledge that without proper nutrition the troops would not function correctly. The kitchen contained enough cooking equipment to prepare any food they wanted. Two large refrigerators, an electric range, gas oven tops, a brick cooking fireplace and a wood fueled boiling fire place.

The living room items were basic; two metal desks, a book case, a video viewer, sofa, two overstuffed black leather chairs and a large picture window that had a view of the street. Their bedrooms contained a twin bed, dressing stand, night stand, dresser, and closet. The closet contained seven workout outfits of purple crop tops and black shorts, seven off-duty summer outfits of black tights and purple tank tops, two semi-formal uniforms of black slacks and formal purple blouses, two formal uniforms of purple skirts, white button up shirts and purple blazers. There were two street walker costumes and two commoner costumes that were used when they went undercover. The dresser held all necessary undergarments, socks, and accessories.

Dakota sat at her desk in her off-duty outfit and went back and forth between the report Prime Minister Boyd had left and the video viewer. She watched video of the various people that the report told her to monitor. Tanna entered the room as she fastened a neckless to finish off her outfit of short white denim shorts, a white barely there top under an unbuttoned white denim vest, She wore tall white boots with high heels. Dakota looked over Tanna as she adjusted her outfit in a mirror, assuring the fit was perfect.

"Nice," Dakota said. "No one will have the ability to resist you. You look just like a walker from the east side where the Alpha men usually get their women from."

"We'll have no trouble destroying a team," Tanna said. "Have you discovered anything useful yet?"

"I have," Dakota said. "I know how we'll get into one of the cells. The leader is a man whose family ran a large manufacturing business before the wars. Under the new rules prohibiting private business ownership, he cannot try to start the business again. I can speak to him like a business owner and that will be our way into that cell."

"Why do you think the Ross Empire outlawed private business ownership?" Tanna asked.

"To prevent people from gaining too much power," Dakota said. "And using that power to hurt others."

"But the emperor has that kind of power," Tanna said.

"He's better than the ordinary person," Dakota said. "I know what you're getting at, believe me, I do. This is one of those things that we simply don't question. He knows best."

"I hope you're right," Tanna said. "Well, I'm off. Don't work too hard."

"You either," Dakota said as she stood still and hugged Tanna before she left.

Dakota watched Tanna walk out of the house before she returned to her work. The more she investigated the rebels, the more they made sense. That fact scared Dakota more than anything else. She knew what happened to people who questioned the government; they disappeared into the night. In her investigations into the Emperor and his family, she found many horrifying facts about the atrocities that had been committed. Dakota wondered why none of the Alpha Troops thought of this but then a thought crossed her mind, *"The Alpha Troops are smart, but nowhere near the level of intelligence of Tanna and me... Could we be too smart for our own good?"*

Chapter #5

There were very few streets left in the country where a woman of such young beauty was able to walk alone and not worry about being raped, kidnapped, or both. The woman was not over eighteen years old and wore flowing light blue baggy pants with a matching sequenced, sparkling, haltered crop top. Her thick, long black hair flowed from the top of her head and barely touched her waistline. She had a light blue mesh scarf veil that covered the majority of her face and allowed her dark brown owl eyes to peer out. There was a sparkle in those eyes, something that told those watching her that the young woman was smiling as she walked quickly down the street.

The woman was in the Charlesville district of Falling Ridge which was the wealthiest district in the city, and possibly the country. Police patrolled the streets and removed anyone who wasn't supposed to be there. As the woman walked past a police car, the cops took note of her, but nothing more, having seen the woman walk down those streets before. They all thought she was nothing more than a private escort girl headed to a school. None of them realized she was the Emperor's main call girl. The woman took no time to look at all the opulent mansions that lined the street. She was on a mission to get to her location.

The woman got to the mansion she was looking for, a red brick mini castle sprawling over the property's two acres. All the houses in this district were designed to resemble mansions built in the late 1800's by the country's rich robber barons. As she walked up the twenty stair marble staircase she didn't take time to appreciate the largest and most magnificent mansion on the street. The police who watched the girl knew that there was nothing strange about a woman entering that house. It had been one of the premier schools in instructing young women on the arts and crafts of love and seduction.

When the woman got to the door she pushed her veil aside and looked into a camera. The person on the other end of the camera looked and when he'd verified it was a member of the school, he unlocked and opened the doors. The girl rushed in the mansion before the doors quickly closed behind her. The mansion was a cool place. Everything was rich and there were dark colors, browns and reds, imported from all over the world. There were other women in the main hallway, waiting for private instructions or tests to begin. The Mediterranean beauty rushed past all of them on her way toward the basement.

The girl entered a room at the northern most end of the house. She locked the door and looked over the room. It was her private office. It had a large wooden mahogany desk with intricate carvings. There was a massive black leather chair, book shelves and cabinets. The woman took off her veil and set it on the desk and paused a moment before she moved to a small vent which had an opening a little over one foot per side. The girl took a deep breath before she lifted the vent cover off and reached inside and tripped a locking mechanism. Once tripped, a wider hole opened around where the vent cover had been. The girl slipped into the wall and closed everything behind her, leaving the room as empty as when she'd entered.

She moved quickly in the dark of the vent shaft. She rushed as she knew there would be nothing in her way. The girl hunched over as she walked in the shaft and saw a single blinking green light. It was dim and at the floor, nearly two hundred feet ahead. She made her way to the light, pushed it in and waited. The wall swung open and the girl rushed into a different room, knowing who would be on the other side.

The room she now stood in was a small office style room with a large window on the opposite side from where she had entered. In the office was a desk with multiple network devises and video viewers. There was one other person in the room, a blonde girl with hawk-like features and piercing eyes. She was not much younger than the one who'd entered. The girl had sun yellow eye shadow that fully covered her eyes and extended in a small band back to her tiny ears as if it were a mask. Her lips had been painted with sparkling silver gloss that instantly attracted attention away from her smooth and perfect skin.

The girl in the room was petite with a short, thin, curvy body that was still developing. She was only sixteen years old but wore the clothing of a well-off commoner who was in their twenties or thirties; deep navy tights, a yellow, haltered crop top, a black sleeveless leather duster, and black fingerless gloves. The only part of her attire that wasn't common was the black military boots that touched up to the bottom of her knees. The woman stood by the large window and looked over to another room. She was facing a sidewall which neither looked out of the window or at the door the girl had come through

When the secret door had fully closed, the girl who stood in the room turned and looked toward the Mediterranean beauty that had entered her office. The girls smiled at one another as they rushed for an embrace.

"Nyx," the blonde said to the Mediterranean concubine as she kissed her once on each cheek. "It's been far too long. So good to see you in the flesh again. Tell me, how goes the fight?"

"Alexis Ross," Nyx said as the girls broke from their embrace. "So much has happened in the past year since we last talked. Your father loses more capacities by the day. He cannot go more than a few hours without sweet leaf. Garret Boyd seizes more power by the day. Charlie is just a figurehead now and the public has no idea. Garret uses Charlie. I'm convinced that Garret is attempting to overthrow the Empire and take it for himself."

"I've suspected that was his play for some time now," Alexis said. "The sound monitoring devices that you installed have given us so much. Look out here," Alexis said as she pointed out the window she'd been standing by. Nyx looked out and saw a large room they were above that contained rows of desks with people listening to headphones and typing on network devices. "My information network is working perfectly. We have infiltrated all levels of the government but have been unable break into Boyd's inner circle. He eludes us."

"He doesn't respond to my women or myself," Nyx said. "I've been close enough to feel him. He's equipped; he's not a eunuch. I had a maid girl spy on him. He would take no women or men. He has no pleasure in his life. I don't understand his motivation. He aspires to take the empire yet has no heirs to pass it to. He has no life other than work."

"There is no greater enemy," Alexis said. "Than the one with no discernable motivation. When motivation is known we can bend them to our will. We don't know his motivation and therefore have no lever to move them with. I have a plan Nyx, but it will put you in great danger."

"I'll give my life for you Alexis," Nyx said. "My family was destroyed by these monsters. I was forced into pleasure houses at an early age. You saved me and gave me a life."

"We need to kill Garret," Alexis said flatly. "He must die. Once he's gone, Charlie will fall. You are so close to him. You have done well in taking the lead role in his life."

"There were many women before me," Nyx said. "But I know how to make a man think of me and only me. I could turn Charlie against Boyd. I may possibly be able to convince Charlie to kill him."

"No," Alexis said. "This has to happen at exactly the right time. I have many supporters in the public and the military but cannot go out because of the price on my head. If we don't act soon the people will forget me. The terrors of the empire cannot continue. We must go back to an elected system. Have you nearly discovered the cure to the amino acids?"

"I have searched," Nyx said. "I have had women and girls search. We stopped a few months ago when one of my younger girls in training was captured and killed. Luckily we didn't tell her what she had been searching for. She was only instructed to find the vaults. They knew someone was searching for something. When I have Charlie in the heat of passion I ask but he doesn't reveal. I use caution as not to draw suspicion.

"We must learn the formula Nyx," Alexis said. "What of the Alpha Troops? We've received reports of a new model that looks like a normal human."

"Beta Troops," Nyx said. "The two they used looked like street walkers. They looked incredibly average but killed with absolute precision. Those Beta Troops could pose the biggest disaster to us. We need to investigate every person that ever tries to join forces with us. We will have no idea if they are the new model of government killer."

"I've always warned," Alexis said. "Just before we have victory all will turn against us. We can win this if we remain vigilant."

"I have a new report though," Nyx said. "This is the report I needed to meet you about. This report is far too hot to trust to a courier."

"Tell me," Alexis said. "What have you discovered?"

"A girl had been kidnapped and taken to a house," Nyx said. "Her brother rescued her. While she was there she told me she works with doctors from the Ridge Medical Center. One of the members of her group works with Alpha and Beta troops. They have a plan to kill a group of Alphas and kidnap two Betas."

"Kidnap them?" Alexis asked. "What would that do?"

"They want to shatter Emperor Ross's sanity," Nyx said. "They want to destroy him and take the empire down. They hope to show them the empire is nothing to fear."

"A very risky gambit," Alexis said as she started to pace. "If it works, the empire will be on higher alert. They will not stop until those behind it are killed. If it doesn't work, they will die in the act of capturing them. I don't see what they will gain by doing this."

"They hope to leverage this," Nyx said. "So they can obtain the formula for the amino acids. They want to give the acid to the people so they no longer must rely on the government."

"Getting people off the amino acid is the first thing we must do," Alexis said. "I have my spy network doing everything they can to find the fourth lab the Freedom Explorers have. Even when I was in my father's graces I was never close to the formula...How do they think they can kill the Alphas? Others have died trying."

"They have a new formula," Nyx said. "It's something that will slow them to the point of death. The group says they have close to one hour of time while the troops will be slowed. That's how they think they'll capture them as well. It is a good plan."

"Not really," Alexis said. "Once Charlie knows someone has this kind of power he will destroy them. Obtain the formula for what they use. I want to know how they intend to stop them. We will monitor their progress and see how it works."

"I will Alexis," Nyx said.

"As for Garret Boyd," Alexis said. "He must die at the most opportune time. If this group succeeds there will be panic and terror in the castle. Charlie will be confused and upset. Then kill Garret."

"Are you sure you have the support to take over?" Nyx asked. "Will the military follow you?"

"Here's where I differ from my predecessors," Alexis said. "Once Boyd is dead and a way to defeat the Alpha Troops is known, I will confront Charlie with you and a light defense force. You will get me into the castle and get Charlie to go to a room and we will work out an agreement. Charlie will step aside and give control to me in exchange for his life. The military will follow command. We'll then destroy the old structure of power and create a new country."

"You make it sound so easy," Nyx said. "But I know what we are up against. Alexis, I will follow you to the depths of hell and back. You can count on me."

"I know I can Nyx," Alexis said. "But there's one more thing."

"What?"

"There is one other secret report that I received," Alexis said. "Not a week ago. I was so glad when you contacted me for a meeting because I knew you would need to hear this."

"What?" Nyx asked. "What is so important?"

"Charlie," Alexis said. "Well, Garret. He knows that I pose the greatest threat to them. They know I am working on destroying the empire and are convinced there are spies in the staff."

"There are," Nyx said. "Many of them gather information and bring it to my network."

"None of them have any contact with you, do they?" Alexis asked.

"Of course not," Nyx answered. "There are precautions in place, levels and layers between my network and I. No one knows who's behind it."

"Good," Alexis said. "Garret is going to gut the staff very soon because he wants to smoke out the leaders of the information dealings. In the report I saw, they don't suspect any of the pleasure women. They investigated you and the school you came from Nyx. They believe you are safe and we have to keep it that way. I'm going to ask you to do one more thing for me."

"Anything."

"Put another layer of distance between yourself and the information," Alexis said. "Keep as far away as possible. You don't want to get pinned with this."

"I'll be careful," Nyx said.

"Stay safe," Alexis said as she moved to Nyx and embraced her. "And move swiftly."

Chapter #6

In the dark of night the air had been heavy with gunshots and police sirens. This is the time people did the things they didn't want seen in broad daylight. The industrial park in the south district of Falling Ridge had always been a hotbed of drug running. The park was situated near the intersection of two interstate highways, two rail lines and near the edge of a harbor. There were hundreds of semis and delivery trucks coming through the area every hour.

The government had always permitted the business managers to allow the activities to continue in the area but the events had spun out of control for nearly two years. In was not uncommon to have three murders a night in the park. The victims were often industrial workers who were just doing their jobs. It rose to the point drivers wouldn't enter the area and the businesses suffered. In a plea to the empire, the workers asked for Alpha Troop patrols. Prime Minister Boyd granted the patrols with strict orders to confiscate all the drugs and weapons so the empire could resell them.

It was a horrible night for everyone at the industrial park. A number of street walkers vied for the men exiting a ship that had been out for over five months. There was a minimal crew onboard but they had their voyage bonus so there would have been plenty for all the women. After the Alpha Troops had sorted the situation out, a massive drug deal went south quickly. Over ten people had died in the crossfire.

A pair of Alpha women walked along a row of shipping containers. The women wore the standard Alpha Troops outfit of a black bodysuit made from smart materials, capable of deflecting a bullet, a helmet, gloves, and boots. The women were massive even by Alpha status. They each stood six feet nine inches tall and had thirty inch biceps. Every part of those women was oversized as they walked along unarmed.

They looked for drug dealers and street walkers. Both troopers knew it was a very dangerous area but they frothed at the mouth to see some heavy action. They sought a massive fight that evening to prove they were the best soldiers. As they walked, a pair of smaller women walked around the corner. The troopers rushed to arrest them, but saw it was Dakota and Tanna dressed in Alpha style battle gear, minus the helmets.

The Alpha Women removed their helmets and saluted them. Dakota had seen the Alpha women with helmets on before but it had always disturbed her how eerily similar the women looked due to genetic engineering. They had dark hair that was stringy and thin that broke at their necklines. Their faces were round and soft with wide set hazel eyes and small noses above a thin mouth and square jaw. Dakota and Tanna saluted the women back. Dakota studied the women, picking up on subtle difference in their appearances; the set of their eyes, the height of the forehead, and the hue of the skin.

"Report," Dakota commanded.

"We've been patrolling this quadrant," one of the Alpha's replied. "This sector is clear."

"Then why have we been hearing gunfire?" Tanna asked.

"That's from the other side of the park ma'am," the Alpha said.

Dakota nodded, noting that like all Alpha groups, only one was allowed to speak. The rest were to stay silent.

"We were told," Dakota said. "That a large shipment of sweet leaf was coming in by rail tonight. How many people have been watching the rail yard?"

"There are four there," the women said. "They are our best men. They've been inspecting all shipments coming in but have yet to find anything suspicious."

"We know something's coming" Tanna said. "Are there any more walkers working this area of the industrial park?"

"We have cleaned them all out," the Alpha woman said. "We made sure they wouldn't be back tonight after the last incident."

"Good," Dakota said. "Keep up the patrol in this quadrant and be ready to rush to the rail yard if backup is needed."

Dakota and Tanna saluted the women who saluted them back as they slipped back into the night and left the Alpha women standing alone.

"I don't like this," the women who spoke to Dakota said.

"What about it?"

"Those two aren't Alpha Troops. Why are they leading us?"

"I have no idea. The orders were to follow all orders they dispensed tonight. They seem to be doing a good job."

"I still don't like it. Alpha Troops should command Alpha Troops. Let's move out."

As the women went to put their helmets back on, two darts sailed out of the darkness and into their necks. They both grabbed their necks and pulled the darts out. They looked at them but had no idea what they were. They tried to step toward the shadows the darts had come from but both of them hit the ground. The women struggled to stand but were so weak they weren't able. They fought with what little strength they had left, but it was no use.

A shadow appeared out of the darkness and brandished a hand gun. The women fought the shadow as it drew nearer, but the shadow rushed up to the women and pressed the gun against one of their heads. The shadow pulled the trigger twice and killed the women one after the other. Two shots to the head all it took to kill Alphas once they'd been weakened by the darts. For the first time ever, two Alpha Troops were killed by civilians. The civilians geared up for the mayhem they planned to create that night.

In the main courtyard in front of a massive industrial building, eight Alpha men stood watch. They wore the standard Alpha uniform of black bodysuits made of smart materials to deflect any bullets. The men had black boots, gloves, helmets, and massive assault rifles. They were almost completely covered from head to toe and had no skin exposed anywhere on their bodies. They were the men getting ready to spring into action as a ship was started to berth at the docks.

From a top level spire above the courtyard, Jerrica aimed her dart gun, a gun that looked like an assault rifle. She had ten darts that contained amino acid pair on the tips loaded into the magazine of the gun. The scope for the gun was almost as long as the barrel. Jerrica tried to still her breath. She knew the instant she hit the first troop others would know something was wrong. She had one chance to get it right.

Jerrica had the sole patch of skin on the back of an Alpha's neck in her view finder when the tiny communicator in her ear crackled to life.

"Jerrica," the female voice said. "Ready?"

"Ready," Jerrica whispered.

Jerrica couldn't see the other shooter but knew the other lady was on a spire on the other side of the courtyard. They were both going to shoot at the same time in hopes to knock out as many as possible. Four shooters were scattered around the targets and prepared to hit the downed troopers with bullets. Jerrica's heart pounded as the communicator crackled back to life.

"Three," the female said. "Two…one…FIRE!!!"

Jerrica pulled the trigger then quickly aimed the gun at the next man in line. She shot and shot again before the Alpha Troops realized what was going on. Jerrica heard guns going off in all directions. She saw seven troops on the ground but many more rushed out of the shadows. The snipers had put multiple bullets into the troops on the ground. From what Jerrica could tell all the downed Alpha Troops had been killed.

As more troops rushed into the courtyard and tried to figure out what happened, Jerrica noticed more of the Alpha Troops falling down. The other woman was still shooting. Jerrica pulled her gun up and continued shooting. Her first two shots both ricocheted off helmets. Her third shot put a woman on the ground. The fourth was deflected by a smart material shirt.

"Jerrica," the female voice said in the communicator. "Get into a hidden position. The bogies are in your building moving toward you. They know. You must hit them in the dark."

"I'm on it," Jerrica said.

Jerrica moved away from the window and back into the room. She was in a storage room that had been filled to capacity with file cabinets and desks. Jerrica looked for a good place to hide and still have a clear view of the door. As she looked, a light in the hallway was turned on. Jerrica knew the Beta Troops were in the hallway. Jerrica thought the best course of action would be to take them quickly.

Jerrica climbed onto a desk near the door so she could maneuver herself behind the door with her back to the wall when the door opened. Jerrica had her gun ready when the door flew open allowing Dakota and Tanna to rush in, looking in the opening of the room, their backs to Jerrica. Jerrica wasted no time in squeezing the trigger. She shot Tanna first since she was standing behind Dakota and quickly followed with a dart into Dakota's neck.

It took more than twice the amount of time for the darts to work on the Betas than on the Alphas, but both Dakota and Tanna hit the floor. Jerrica jumped down from the desk and pulled a pistol off her belt. She aimed it at the girls who writhed in pain on the floor. Jerrica wasn't sure how long the darts would last on the Betas but she wasn't going to take any chances. Dakota was trying to stand but didn't have the strength to pull herself up.

"What...did...you...do...to...us?" Dakota asked as she struggled to spit every word out.

Tanna was clutching at her chest. Her heart beat so fast Tanna thought that it would explode. A pain spider webbed out from her heart, through her chest, like her blood and organs were slowed down running through mud. They tried to fight it, but were limp on the floor.

"I made you weak," Jerrica said. "That's the only way the empire will fall. This is the only way Emperor Ross II will end his reign of terror. There are dead Alpha Troops in the courtyard. You think he'll listen to us now? If he doesn't we'll take every one of you out."

"Can't...get...away," Dakota sputtered as she still tried to stand.

Dakota tried to use a desk to pull herself up and get to her feet; trying to stand on her legs but she couldn't walk. Jerrica watched her attempt to advance toward her. Tanna was on the floor still unable to move and losing the ability to breathe. Jerrica walked up to Dakota and with one punch, sent her crashing back down to the ground.

"Conserve your strength," Jerrica said. "We aren't sure how many side effects this could have on you. You'll need everything you've got to fight this. We don't want to kill you. We are going to take you with us. Everything will be okay and your names will forever be remembered for your help in bringing down the empire."

Dakota tried to stand up and scream at Jerrica. She didn't want to be in this state; powerless, helpless, and pathetic. Two men, Bradly and Aaron, members of the resistance, pushed a cart through the door. They quickly loaded Dakota and Tanna on the cart and left the room. Jerrica and the two men rushed through the building as Jerrica kept the gun aimed at the Beta Troops the entire time.

Near the rear of the building was a transport vehicle with the engine running. The truck had been prepped for that moment. Jerrica threw the rear doors open and helped the men load Dakota and Tanna in the back. Bradly rushed to the driver's door and got in while Aaron and Jerrica got in back and closed the doors as Alpha Troops ran toward the vehicle.

The vehicle spun its tires and ripped out of the parking area. As the transport took off, all the Alpha Troops opened fire. A commander barked orders to stop the vehicle from leaving the area. The transport turned on the main exit and picked up speed as a truck veered in front of it. The vehicle smashed into the truck and rolled. It stopped just shy of the exit to the industrial park.

Alpha Troops stormed the transport and ripped the doors off. They were stunned at what they saw. The transport was empty, no bodies at all. There was a bank of electronics, wires and servos to operate the machine by satellite. They noticed a large hole in the bottom of the vehicle and rushed back to where the transport had sat outside the building, only to find a manhole cover. One of the Alpha men pulled the cover off and saw yet another cover. The second cover was made of steel and had steel locking mechanisms that kept it in place. Four Alpha men attempted to pull the cover off but were unable budge it. The cover would need to be cut out with a plasma cutter.

The Alpha Troops returned to the courtyard to report to their commanders what had happened. They looked around at all the carnage that had happened so quickly. Alpha Troops were dead on the ground and the two new Beta Troops had been captured. Every Alpha Troop that was there knew they would be disciplined for what happened. They also knew the empire was vulnerable for the first time ever.

Chapter #7

As Dakota was pushed into the van she suddenly felt herself falling down a hole. The entire experience had been like a dream. Dakota could almost see herself falling and being captured. She couldn't estimate how long the fall was, but the landing was soft, into a net that caught her like a fluffy cloud. She instantly felt a pair of hands on her that pulled her off the net an instant before Tanna fell into the net. In the darkness Dakota was unable to tell how many people were around the net, only that every time someone landed, people quickly pulled them out of the way.

Dakota tried to gain some bearings as to where she was. She smelled sewage and heard water gently running like in a small stream, moving over rocks. Dakota observed they were in a dank and dark brick tunnel near a sewer system. The lights were dim with just enough to see rats run along the edges of the bricks. Dakota felt herself being lifted and placed on a bench. The bench seemed to slowly rock up and down in a fluid, gentle motion. Dakota could only assume that they had a boat in the drainage system; that being the only way this group could get away without being seen.

Tanna was thrown into the boat next to Dakota in a way that left their bodies touching one another. Dakota turned her head and saw Tanna's eyes open but completely glassed over. Her eyes weren't focusing on anything. She stared blankly at the bottom of the boat. Dakota heard the engine start and saw a man in a gray suit sitting at the wheel of the boat. As the boat started to move forward, Dakota could feel her consciousness slipping away as everything went black.

Dakota awoke before she opened her eyes. She'd never felt so horrible. Every part of her body throbbed with pain like she'd been throttled in a street fight. Dakota felt tired but didn't want to fall back asleep. It took her a moment to comprehend she was on the floor and stripped down to her underwear which left her completely exposed. The room was cold and the concrete ground was hard as it pressed against her back. No sounds could be heard in the room. Dakota felt a hand on her side, shaking her.

"Dakota," Tanna whispered. "Dakota, please, are you okay?"

"Tanna," Dakota said. "I'm here."

Dakota opened her eyes and looked around the room and saw Tanna. Tanna's hair was a mess and she had been stripped as well. The room was a square with concrete walls and no windows. There was nothing in the room save a small door on one side. The room was illuminated by a single bulb that hung from the ceiling. Dakota tried to look over her body to see if there was any bruising or damage but her eyes couldn't focus. There was a haze in her mind she just couldn't shake.

"Why is this happening Dakota?" Tanna asked through tears. "What did we do wrong?"

"I don't know Tanna," Dakota said trying to get her mind together. "Someone wants to destroy the government and take down the empire. We are casualties in a war."

"I don't want to die," Tanna said. "What are we going to do?"

"I don't know," Dakota said. "Can you stand?"

"No," Tanna said trying. "Every muscle in by body is on fire. I can't focus. There is pain that I cannot describe. I feel like I've spent a week in the fighting arena. Every muscle is throbbing like I've been beaten up."

"Same here," Dakota said.

"Are we going to join them?" Tanna asked.

"WHAT?" Dakota screamed.

"Join them," Tanna said. "They may force us to join them or die. Do we join them?"

"We die," Dakota said. "We are fighters for the empire. There is nothing they can do to cause me to join with someone on a mission to destroy the empire."

"I will stand beside you Dakota," Tanna said. "It's your decision."

"You want to betray the empire?" Dakota asked.

"We saw what happened the other night," Tanna said. "The Emperor has two sets of rules; one for the people and one for himself. He sells drugs and kills the people who buy them. He confiscates them and resells them or uses them himself. There are so many people who have vanished in the night."

"He's a good man at heart," Dakota said.

"No he's not," Tanna said. "If he was he'd share the formula for the amino acid so there would be no forced death. Emperor Ross II wants total control and won't allow anyone to live a life of their choice."

"I don't believe that," Dakota said.

Dakota was about to continue when the door to the room opened and four people enter the room; Jerrica and Doctor Prowl with Bradly and Aaron as guards. Dakota couldn't make them out from her limited view on the floor. Her eyes still wouldn't focus. Dakota had no idea of how long they'd been there or what was about to happen. The people who entered the room carried chairs with them. They set them against the back wall and lifted each of the girls into their own chairs. They cuffed the girls into the chairs and linked the cuffs to bolts that were secured in the concrete wall.

A man moved in close to Dakota and flashed a light in her eyes. Dakota decided to stay silent instead of yelling at them or telling them how much trouble they would be in. She felt something prick her neck and things immediately became much clearer. There was a man and woman in the room who Dakota had never seen before. They were dressed professionally in business suits along with two guards in business suits who held large handguns.

"As you can see," the woman said in a soft voice. "We no longer fear you."

Jerrica looked at the two young women that had been locked into the chairs. Doctor Prowl was beside them checking their vital signs to make sure there was no damage. Jerrica waited for one of the women to speak but they never did. Jerrica smiled.

"Cat got your tongue?" Jerrica asked. "No matter. We killed many of the Alpha Troops that were in the industrial park tonight. They didn't last against us. We've shown Emperor Ross II that he no longer controls the country."

"You poor pathetic fool!" Dakota exclaimed. "Do you realize the vengeance Emperor Ross II will level upon the country? He will kill until he's smoked out all of your resistance and you'll be publicly tortured and executed."

"That's exactly what we want," Jerrica said matter of factly as Monte moved away from them.

"Are you out of your mind?" Dakota asked as she tried to wrap her mind around what Jerrica had said. "You have sealed your death warrant. There will be a price on your head. You will be hunted like rabbits and Emperor Ross II will not allow you to live."

"What you fail to realize," Jerrica said. "Is that we want Ross II to overreact. We want him to cause suffering. You see, the people have reached their tipping point. They are tired of being ruled. The people want the country the way it was when it was first formed. They want to be able to carve their own paths. They are tired of government instructing them on every aspect of their lives. With the retaliation that Ross II will unleash, the people are sure to revolt. They will not stand for it any longer. That's why we did this. Ross II has to act but there's nothing he can do anymore."

"You will not receive the amino acids," Dakota said. "He will withhold them and you will die a slow and painful death."

"That's where you come in," Jerrica said. "We've been trying to develop the amino acid to prevent the deaths that come with it. The amino acids have been engineered to be so complex we cannot break them down and synthesize them for ourselves."

"What does that have to do with us?" Dakota asked.

"You will get us the formula," Jerrica said. "It will be the price for your lives. We know what you are and what they've done to you. We know how you've been trained and what you are capable of. You will get us the formula."

"I will do no such thing," Dakota said. "We refuse to help monsters like you."

"Then you choose to die," Jerrica said. "Doctor, kill them."

Doctor Prowl moved toward the girls with a syringe in his hand. Monte was prepared to inject Dakota with the liquid in the needle.

"STOP!" Tanna shouted. "Please, don't hurt her. I'll do anything."

Doctor Prowl froze and looked at Jerrica. Jerrica smiled and motioned him back.

"Our intelligence on you was perfect," Jerrica said.

"Intelligence?" Dakota asked.

"That you two have worked and trained together from the start," Jerrica said. "There are things unknown to us but we've learned enough. You do all your training in pairs to create an intense bond. That bond will cause you to do anything to prevent pain or harm to the other. That's how we'll break you."

"Die and burn in hell," Dakota shouted as she spit in Jerrica's face. "Kill me you coward. You got the guts for that? I will make sure you suffer before you die."

"Threaten all you want," Jerrica said. "We need to know all your secrets. We took DNA samples in the twenty minutes you were passed out. Our tests worked perfectly, showed us exactly what you are and how to kill you. I'm actually going to let you walk out of here. You will get the formula for the amino acids and when a person from my group finds you, you will give it to them. That's the deal. We know how to find you and we know how to take you out if you refuse."

"I refuse," Dakota said. "I will not betray the emperor. You will never get away with this. I'm sure the Alpha Troops are already on their way to us. We have trackers built into our skin. The satellites know exactly where we are at."

"Which is why," Jerrica smiled. "We took you into the drainage system before we brought you here. They lost your signal. This room is four-foot-thick concrete. There's no way your satellite tracker signal could be picked up in here."

Dakota considered what Jerrica was saying. She had seen how the Alpha Troops were dying that night. She knew how easily she and Tanna had been captured. Dakota knew they were in grave trouble. She didn't care if she died, but as Jerrica had predicted, Dakota would do everything in her power to prevent anything from happening to Tanna. Dakota tried to test her chains. She knew she should be more than strong enough to pull them out of the wall but as she struggled with it, Dakota realized she wasn't anywhere near powerful.

"Your full strength won't return for another hour or so," Jerrica said as she noticed Dakota's determination. "At that point you can rip the chains out of the wall and simply walk away. You'll be contacted within two weeks by a member of my group to deliver the amino acid formula. If you don't have the formula you will be forced to take turns watching the other suffer."

Jerrica smiled again as she and Monte walked out of the room and closed the door behind them. Dakota and Tanna pulled on their chains but nothing worked, they were far too weak. The girls stopped trying and settled in to wait for the chemicals to wear off.

"What's our play then?" Tanna asked. "What can we do from here?"

"When we get out of here," Dakota said. "We go to Emperor Ross II and Prime Minister Boyd. We tell them everything we know. We'll explain how the Alpha Troops were taken out."

"What do you think they'll do" Tanna asked.

"I have no idea," Dakota said. "There are no good answers. Hopefully when they check us over they will determine what we were injected with. If they pinpoint what made us weak, they can develop something to counter it."

"And if they can't counter it?" Tanna asked.

"Then we may have to come up with a new plan."

Chapter #8

Dakota and Tanna remained locked up for over an hour. They meditated while they were detained. After an hour, Dakota broke out of her cuffs with very little effort. Tanna followed suit. Dakota moved to the locked door and used her abnormal strength to break through the concrete door. The girls entered an empty concrete hallway. It was dark and dank with pools of water on the floor.

"What do we do?" Tanna asked.

"We go directly to Emperor Ross II and tell him what happened," Dakota said. "He must know. This new threat could destroy the empire. He must be prepared."

"The day may have arrived," Tanna said. "Everything that goes up must come down Dakota. The Ross Empire might be in its final days. This is the obvious outcome we are staring in the face."

"Where is this coming from Tanna?" Dakota asked. "We are sworn to protect the empire, not hand it over to rebels."

"My mind won't stop racing," Tanna said. "I look at all the data that is available and this is the computation that I've come to. There are so many people who are upset and no change can be made. Fundamentally, the human race needs change. Complacency is death to them. They can handle it for a little while but soon need to be shaken. I feel there is no way the empire can survive. Very soon the people will revolt. We can join them and be in the first wave of the new empire."

"That's treason," Dakota said firmly. "I love you Tanna but we cannot turn our backs on Emperor Ross II and his empire. It is the way of things. Do not even breathe a word of this again. If you do, I will take you before Emperor Ross II and you answer for your crime."

"I understand," Tanna said. "If you feel that strongly, I won't mention it again."

"Good," Dakota said. "Now follow me."

Dakota took off running, upset by the conversation she'd just had. She couldn't figure out how Tanna could even begin to think such things. Dakota knew she had to keep a very sharp eye on Tanna to make sure that she didn't act on any of those ideas. She knew everything Tanna had said was true but they had sworn to protect the emperor and every empire goes through difficult times and the Ross Empire was no different, they would get through this threat as they'd gotten through others; with a unified front.

The girls made it out of the building and looked around. It took Dakota only a few seconds to gain her bearings. She realized they were northwest of the castle by abut ten miles. Dakota motioned to Tanna and the girls ran. They ran at speeds thought impossible by humans and Alpha Troops alike. Dakota and Tanna ran so fast they made it to the outer grounds of the castle complex in just below ten minutes.

The girls ran past their house and used the back entrances to the castle which gave them access to the castle without having to go through extra security. The girls took no time to stop and put something on over their underwear. They were intent on getting to Emperor Ross II as quickly as possible to tell him what they'd uncovered.

In the castle the girls were directed to a small office. They each took a chair in the small room that only had a few chairs and one table, a portrait of the castle on the wall and a large globe atop a tall pedestal. The sole window in the room looked out over the courtyard of the castle. They were on the second floor but took no time to look out over the beautiful landscaping outside the window.

Both Dakota and Tanna stood at attention and saluted when Emperor Ross II and Prime Minister Boyd entered the room. Both men looked stressed. The Emperor wore a fancy purple robe, ornate and tied tight. Garret was wearing military trousers with a mismatched button down shirt. It was obvious the pair had been woken in the night with reports of the Alpha Troops having been killed. Emperor Ross II saluted back and motioned for them to sit down.

"At ease," Charlie said.

"Sorry for appearing out of uniform," Dakota said. "And for being so exposed in front of you."

"There's nothing to apologize for," Charlie said as he eyed the women. "You look so lovely. I hope you weren't hurt in action tonight."

"WHAT HAPPENED?" Garret yelled as he paced around the room. "They really killed Alpha Troops tonight?"

"They did," Dakota said. "From what we could tell they hit the troops in an exposed patch of skin with a dart. The dart was tainted with something that caused the Alpha Troops to slow and be weakened. Once in a debilitated state, they were shot."

"Why didn't you stop them?" Garret demanded. "And why did it take so long to bring these reports to us? There could have been more damage done."

"We caught a glistening of light off the barrel of a gun," Tanna said. "In an upper level spire. We raced up to apprehend the party with the gun but we were attacked with the darts. We were taken to a secure location where we were given information about what was going on."

"What was going on?" Garret asked.

"They are making a move for the empire," Dakota said. "They want to demonstrate they no longer fear you. They want to show you your Alpha Troops are no longer untouchable."

"Who were they?" Garret asked.

"No idea sir," Dakota said. "We were in a concrete room about ten miles northwest of here. There was a man and a woman with armed guards. The woman did the talking. She was not much older than we are. There were no markings on their attire to indicate where their loyalty lied. I would venture a guess they are doctors with advanced knowledge of genetics and genetic engineering. The darts we were hit with thickened our blood."

"They thickened your blood?" Charlie asked. "What good would that do?"

"One difference between the Alpha Troops and humans," Dakota said. "Is that our blood vessels are tripled in size allowing more blood and oxygen to reach the muscles and brain. It increases all functions. Thickening the blood slowed the flow of the blood; hence, slowing us down. Our hearts needed to work much harder to push the blood through and therefore used most of the available energy in our bodies. They shot the Alpha Troops in their heads which destroyed the brain while their repair functions were occupied with trying to thin the blood."

"Unreal," Garret said. "For this to take place they would have to know the secrets of the Alpha Troops. They couldn't have blindly guessed in the night."

"Not necessarily," Tanna said. "If a human were to be hit with one of those darts they would most certainly die within seconds. The blood would congeal in their heart. This group could have just guessed that thickening the blood would work."

"That's not what I meant Tanna," Garret said. "We developed that very system to kill Alpha Troops when we first created them."

"Why?" Dakota asked. "Why would you ever need to kill your own troops?"

"Two reasons," Garret said as Charlie looked on, bored. "First, if a Troop was somehow captured and their genetics were investigated, someone could replicate the technology. If they did, we would have a readymade way to kill them."

"That makes sense," Tanna said.

"What's the second reason?" Dakota asked.

"Second," Garret said. "Was if the Alpha Troops ever tried turning on us. If a riot or revolt were ever to take place, we knew we would need a way to put them down quickly. The fact someone used our exact technique makes me wonder who within the empire is working to bring us down. This cannot stand. Charlie, we need action and we need it now."

"Again," Charlie whined. "I don't care. I was in a nice warm bed with my favorite girl Nyx when you woke me up and bothered me with this dribble. I don't care. I want to go back to bed."

Dakota couldn't believe what she was hearing. She had put so much faith into Emperor Ross II and hearing him say he didn't care about his people shattered all of her convictions. In that moment, for the first time ever, she wondered if Tanna was right. That thought only lasted a moment before she pushed it out of her head. Emperor Ross II was their leader and they had to follow him.

"I've got a plan," Garret said. "It has been in the books for some time now. There's a community that's been very noisy about the way the empire's run. They want change. They want to strip our power and besmirch the Ross name. We will take that community and blame them for the attack. People will demand action and we will give it to them. We will show them our ruthlessness. We will withhold the amino acid to the community."

"You're going to kill them all?" Dakota asked.

"They deserve to die," Garret said. "They have been a problem for some time now. This will show everyone what happens when we are defied and will get rid of those who constantly push us."

"But there will be innocents in that community," Tanna said. "How can you kill innocent people? Children?"

"It's easy knowing they are dying to preserve the integrity of the country," Garret said. "They will die to protect us. It's really an honor they do not deserve."

"I cannot believe what I'm hearing," Tanna said. "It's wrong."

"Did you just make a moral judgment?" Garret asked as he got closer to Tanna. "Did you criticize something your government... your emperor has decided?"

"What I meant," Tanna said as she stuttered upon realizing she had over stepped her bounds.

"I don't care what you meant," Garret said.

Garret moved closer to Tanna before he reached into his pocket and pulled out a small blade. Garret drove the blade into the back of Tanna's neck. Tanna screamed in pain as everyone perked up. Tanna pulled the blade out and began to shake. She fell to her knees before her entire body fell flat on the ground. She shook. It had all happened so fast that Dakota and Charlie didn't know how to react. Garret had another knife in his hand and pointed it at Dakota.

"Are you with us or against us?" Garret rumbled with fire intensity in his eyes.

"With you," Dakota screamed. "I've always been with you. Please."

"Then you are safe," Garret said. "As for your friend..."

Garret pulled a third knife from his pocket. He bent down and slashed Tanna across the throat. She died instantly. Dakota recoiled in horror at seeing her friend and Beta Troop partner lying dead on the floor. Dakota didn't know what to say or how to react.

"I hope you take this as a lesson," Garret said. "We will not be subverted. Those who think they can defeat us have another thing coming."

"What happens now?" Dakota asked. "I need a partner."

"You will spend some time in jail," Garret said. "As a reminder. You will be given a new partner there. You will have to train her. When you two are released from jail you will be given a mission. This has to be done."

"It will," Dakota said. "I think this is a good idea. I have some things I know I need to train on and improve. Training a new partner will be good for me. It will sharpen my skills."

"I hope so," Garret said. "I have big plans for you and I'd hate to have to slit your throat as well."

Garret called two guards into the room. The guards entered and he handed them the knife he still had in his hand.

"Take this woman to the jail under the castle," Garret said. "She is to be placed under the heaviest security. Every precaution must be put in place. I want four Alpha Troops guarding her at all times. They are to remain outside the hallway door and if she tries to escape, kill her. If she gives you any trouble, stab her with that knife."

The guards took Dakota and escorted her out of the room. Charlie barely looked up from his sitting position while Garret paced around the room. Garret's face was frozen in a contemplating gaze. Charlie finally had to break the silence of the room.

"Why did you put her under the castle?" Charlie asked. "With guards outside the hallway?"

"To see if she tries to escape," Garret said.

"That makes no sense," Charlie said.

"It does Charlie," Garret said. "Look, the other had visions of opposing us. The one thing I've feared about Beta Troops is we have made them much too smart for our purposes. The cell has monitoring devices and we will be aware of any attempts to escape. We'll give it one week. If Dakota behaves and is loyal to us, we'll give her a new partner and send them back out on the streets. If not, she, along with the other Beta Troops we have prepared, will be terminated and we'll have to make adjustments to the program."

"Wonderful," Charlie said standing. "I'm returning to bed."

Charlie exited the room and left Garret by himself. Garret shook his head at Charlie's lack of interest in such delicate matters. Garret knew Charlie had no convictions to continue acting as leader. He knew very soon his plans would have to include finding a way to remove Charlie as Emperor and insert himself as ruler of U-Cam.

Chapter #9

The room was filled with a number of video viewers all tuned to different news stations talking about the recent attacks on the Alpha Troops. Every station in the country had reported the story of the terrorist group that had launched an attack against the Emperor. Emperor Ross II had given a press conference assuring his people the guilty parties were known and would be dealt with in swift fashion. The news networks were just beginning to report on the destruction that had been caused by the empire not one week after they had been humiliated.

Watching the reports with his eyes glued to the viewers, was Adam Plains. When he'd first heard retaliation was coming he feared for his life. He thought it might be best to go to the Emperor and beg his forgiveness. He knew he couldn't. The best he could hope for would be a quick death for himself and his friends. Adam knew he had to stay with them.

As Adam continued to watch the announcement, the door to the room opened and Doctors Kent and Prowl walked in with Jerrica and another woman Adam had never seen. The strange woman was beautiful though, dark skin with black hair, pouty lips and perfect skin. She was dressed like an ancient Egyptian princess but Adam knew why. The woman moved with the body awareness of a highly trained courtesan who had been well instructed in pleasuring men. The costume was probably requested by a client but Adam couldn't imagine Chas or Monte hiring such a woman.

"What have the news feeds been saying Adam?" Monte asked.

"Same as before," Adam replied eyeing the woman. "They estimate the entire community of ten thousand people died. Emperor Ross II cut off their supply of the amino acids and let nature take its course."

"There's nothing natural about it," Doctor Kent said. "Abomination is what it really is. The Ross family name needs to be blackened from history for this."

"Who is this girl though?" Adam asked. "And why is she here?"

"This is Nyx," Doctor Kent said. "She's the emperor's main concubine. One he uses almost every day now."

"And why is she here?" Adam asked.

"I'm here," Nyx replied. "To help you take down the emperor."

"Why?" Adam asked. "Why do you want him taken down and why are you helping us?"

"First of all," Nyx said. "You're helping me. Let's get that straight right from the start. Second, I've seen the horrors of Charlie and Garret. They have no value for human life. The way they see it, the subjects of this country are here to serve and benefit them. You have no idea how many women Charlie went through before I came along. My family used to be very well off until the Emperor thought we were too wealthy so he confiscated everything. He killed my parents and brother, forcing me to watch, before he put me into one of his pleasure schools. I was only ten at the time. I swore revenge that same day."

"If you want revenge," Adam asked. "Why don't you kill him when he falls asleep? Why don't you destroy him in the night, quick and easy?"

"Garret needs to be destroyed too," Nyx said. "And the entire empire system. Most think they could cut the head off the snake and the body would die but that's not true. Kill Charlie and a new person steps up. He still has sons that are capable. No. For this to work the entire structure of the empire must be sent crashing down and to avoid unending chaos we need to have a ruler and a system in place to guide the population through the change."

"Where would the change end?" Adam asked.

"With full elections for a government," Nyx said. "We would build a government in which no single person would have total power. It would be a system where people's voices will be heard. This is the only way our country can return to glory."

"Sounds like a dream," Adam said. "Who's going to lead them, you?"

"No," Nyx said. "Someone I work with though. They knew my story and came to save me. A person who instructed me in the schools. That's not what I'm here to talk to you about though. I need to know about your system for defeating the Alpha Troops."

"How do you know it was us?" Adam asked standing.

"Calm down Adam," Doctor Kent said. "She's been working with me for some time now. We thicken their blood to slow them down. They aren't able to fight or heal themselves and that enables us to kill them. The system worked perfectly. We even caught the two new Beta Troops."

"They killed one of them," Nyx said flatly. "They killed her after questioning her. The other is locked in a cell right now. They are keeping her locked up to see if she harbors the same anti-empire thoughts her former partner did. Once they are sure she doesn't they will give her a new partner to train. They didn't count on how intelligent they really made them. This girl is very uncertain about how the empire is working right now. It wouldn't take much to get her on our side."

"Our main goal," Jerrica said. "Is finding the amino acid formula. We must discover how to manufacture the proteins ourselves. Once we do, everyone will be willing to stand against the empire. That must be the primary goal."

"It is," Doctor Kent said. "We must discover where the amino acids are being made. If we can get her on our side we can use her to break in and steal it. Even if the place is guarded with Alpha Troops we have ways of dealing with them."

"That's a good plan," Nyx said. "But even I haven't been able to get that information and I've been trying for years. Emperor Ross II is very quiet about it. I actually wonder if he even knows. Prime Minister Boyd may be the only one and I cannot crack him. Garret won't say a word to me."

"If we could get the Beta Troops on our side," Monte said. "They could access it by force."

"Then our intentions will be known," Doctor Kent said. "We must focus on staying off the radar for as long as we can."

"There is one other option," Nyx said. "Everyone knows the legend of a rumored fourth lab. The Freedom Explorers had the formula hidden somewhere else. They had sought out the lab since the empire was created and have never discovered it."

"Because it doesn't exist," Adam said. "Simply a legend. There are always legends and rumors and mysteries about groups like the Freedom Explorers."

"Something tells me there's more to it than that," Jerrica said. "Or else why spend all the time and money looking for it?"

"That's right," Nyx said. "The reason the first Emperor Ross even knew about it was he had captured and tortured a member of the Freedom Explorers. Ross had information about four labs but couldn't find the fourth. The freedom fighter confirmed a fourth lab did indeed exist and that the formula for both the Shackle Virus and the amino acid to cure it was there.

The biggest secret of the fourth lab was rumored to have been a permanent cure. We would never need the manufactured amino acid again."

"They told the emperor this?" Adam asked. "Incredible."

"They had her baby," Nyx said. "Emperor Ross held a threat over the child. The woman didn't want to see her daughter put into the schools to be a street walker. The life those girls lead is empty, alone, and short. Those who don't overdose or die on drugs usually get beaten to death or die alone in the streets. The average life expectancy for one of those women is only twenty-five."

"It's a horrible crime," Doctor Kent said. "Something we will have to rid ourselves of. Bring morality and decency back to this country."

"But the formula," Jerrica said. "We wouldn't be reliant on the empire? If that were released no one would fear them. But tell me, they've been searching for this lab for years now, how are we supposed to find it when they couldn't? If it even exists.

"What do you mean?" Adam asked.

"Think about it," Jerrica said. "They were going to do unimaginable harm to her daughter if she didn't tell them about the fourth lab, so what if she just made up the story? They haven't found it, so who's to know?"

"What happened to her?" Doctor Prowl asked.

"She was forced to reveal the location," Nyx said. "They locked her away with her baby while they searched it out. The woman killed her daughter then herself before they returned."

"She made it up," Adam said.

"I don't think so," Nyx said.

"Then why didn't they find it?" Adam asked

"The woman was my grandmother," Nyx said. "They put a baby in the cell with her but it wasn't her daughter. They had been giving her drugs so she wouldn't be in her right mind. Emperor Ross did exactly what he said he would. He put my mother into the schools but those who remained loyal to her family got her out. She was married and had children. The family prospered. Once they got too much wealth, they were killed and I was placed in the schools. I was saved though, but not before I became one of the best. As a twist, the emperor wanted to make sure I was trained to serve only him, so I got more training than any of the other girls did. With my education and the training I received from a mentor who wants to see this government taken down, I was able to insert myself as Emperor Ross II's favorite girl. I got rid of all the others and he now trusts me completely."

"But that still leaves us with the fact that there's no way to discover where the fourth lab is," Adam said.

"There's one more thing you need to know," Nyx said. "Within my family's house the emperor confiscated, there was a hidden vault. In that vault are all the details about the location and conditions of the fourth lab."

There were gasps around the room. Nyx was basically handing them the formula to bring down the government and hadn't yet asked for anything in return. The doctors were excited by the prospects of being able to find the lab.

"Why haven't you used this before?" Adam asked. "Why now? Why us?"

"I haven't used this before," Nyx said. "Because I haven't discovered a group before that was capable of pulling this off. You have the ability to take down the Alpha Troops and

I have the backing of someone who can seamlessly take control of the government and bring about the changes we need. I could have exposed this before but we weren't in position to capitalize on it."

"Who is your backer?" Adam asked. "Who do you work with?"

"Alexis Ross," Nyx said. "The daughter of Emperor Ross II."

"Another Ross," Adam said. "The guard changes but the names remain the same."

"Not Alexis," Nyx said. "She will be different. Alexis will not take the mantle of emperor. She will hold elections. Alexis will give everyone the amino acid so they no longer are forced to rely on the government."

"What's our play Nyx?" Doctor Kent asked. "Anything you need we will provide. How do we use this to our fullest advantage?"

"Our ploy is to continue what you placed in motion," Nyx said. "We must take the Beta Troops and attempt to get them to our side. In due time I will go to the vault and discover the location of the lab. I don't want to know the location until we are ready to go in case they try any kind of torture on me. I can't tell them where the lab is if I don't know the real location."

"We must move very carefully," Doctor Prowl said. "The emperor's guard is up. He knows we have power and can stand against his troops. This attack against the community may have been the first of many. We have to be careful."

"And we will," Jerrica said. "Monte, are you ready to attempt to turn the Beta Troops?"

"I am," Monte said. "I'm confident that they will join us. If they turn me down I will make sure their deaths are swift and painless."

Chapter #10

The air was warm and moist making the dimly lit brick walls appear to be sweating as Dakota sat alone in her cell. She waited for news of her fate. The cell was large with a pair of workout machines. There was a communicator to order any food she wanted. Dakota hadn't seen anyone since she'd been placed in the cell. Her food was delivered through a side opening so she never saw who brought the nutrition to her.

Dakota picked at her pasta dish that contained sautéed hare with a rich, creamy sauce. The door opened and a girl no more than fifteen years old was pushed in and the door snapped shut. The girl wore the same outfit as Dakota, a purple sleeveless crop top and black tights. The girl stood short and stocky and was barely over five feet tall with muscular legs and arms coming out of a solid, powerful frame.

Dakota looked over the girl. Her face was narrow with a regal forehead and high cheekbones framed out by silver, glittering hair that was bobbed to her shoulders and square around her face. The tiny eyes were light blue, sunk deep into the face, shrouded by long, elegant eyelashes. The tiny mouth with ruby red lips concealed perfect teeth and was drawn into a wry smile. The girl's skin was pale and fair without a single blemish. The girl smiled at Dakota.

"I guess you're the one who will finish my training," she said in a soft, haunting voice. "I'm called September."

"That's an interesting name," Dakota said. "I'm Crystal Dakota but I go by Dakota. How much training do you have?"

"I've had a lot," September said as she motioned Dakota to go near her. "Test me and find out. We'll see who can take the other down first."

September moved into a fighting position while Dakota walked up to her. Dakota and September squared up and moved toward each other. They locked up and struggled for a quick takedown. They moved around the cell and Dakota pushed September back against a wall. September tried to push back but Dakota was far stronger. Dakota twisted quickly and in the blink of an eye, September was on her back with Dakota's leg across her throat. Dakota held her in position for a moment, just long enough for September to realize she'd been defeated. Dakota stood and helped September up.

"You are good," Dakota said. "You've been trained well but there's a lot of training you still need. What areas did your last trainers focus on?"

"We focused on weapons training," September said. "I learned how to kill with any type of weapon or how to use anything as a weapon. I didn't receive much hand to hand fighting."

"How about strength training?" Dakota asked.

"I'm about half the strength of the average Alpha Troop woman," September said. "You are much stronger than I am."

"That will be the first thing we work on," Dakota said. "You need to be stronger."

"What will our first mission be?" September asked.

"Don't get ahead of yourself," Dakota said. "We first have to earn the right to get out of this prison. My last partner was killed because of her view of the empire."

"She was against it?" September asked.

"Parts of it," Dakota said. "I have to agree holding the population hostage with the amino acid is not ideal but it's what the emperor needs to do to keep the peace within the country."

"I've only been in training my entire life," September said. "I've never been out within the country. I couldn't imagine some of the things the empire does. I heard you were attacked and taken by a group that can counter the Alpha Troops."

"We were," Dakota said. "We were completely helpless. There was nothing that we could do to counter the drugs that they had injected us with. I felt so helpless and weak."

"I couldn't imagine anything like that," September said. "Did the attackers gain anything with their attack?"

"They showed Emperor Ross II they are not afraid of the empire," Dakota said. "They tried to make a bargain with us. We were told to get the formula for the amino acid so they could make it and break the empire's stranglehold on the people. They told us we would soon be contacted again and given a choice. We either acquire the formula or we will be destroyed along with all the Alpha Troops."

"What are you going to do?" September asked.

"Fight until I win or die," Dakota said. "I will not betray the empire."

"Even after what they've done to your partner?" September asked. "What they've done to the people?"

"I don't know," Dakota said. "I'm so confused. I don't understand what I'm feeling or thinking. I hate what they are doing but I could never do anything to harm the emperor or his empire."

The girls were about to continue their conversation when the cell door opened. A dignified doctor entered the room in a white lab coat he wore over a three piece gray suit. He carried a silver metal briefcase that had multiple locking systems keeping it closed. Both girls moved to the far side of the cell as the door closed and locked behind the doctor. Dakota instantly recognized the doctor as the one who'd been in the room with Tanna and her when they were captured.

"You again," Dakota said. "What do you want?"

"It is time for you to make a decision," Doctor Prowl said. "I represent a group that wants to rid the world of this empire. We need your help. You can join us now or I will kill you."

"I've been in this cell since you let us go," Dakota said. "I never even had a chance to look for the formula."

"I know" Doctor Prowl said. "Did you hear an entire community was blamed for the attack on the Alpha Troops?"

"No," Dakota said.

"Over ten thousand innocent people died," Doctor Prowl said. "All because Emperor Ross II is concerned about losing any power. The loss of life with this empire is staggering."

"I didn't know," Dakota said. "How did they choose which community to kill?"

"The community had asked for elections," Doctor Prowl said. "They wanted a representative government like this country use to have. They didn't want one person to have so much control."

"That's terrible," Dakota said. "But part of the empire."

"You condone it then?" Monte asked.

"No," Dakota said.

"But you support it," Doctor Prowl said. "And allow it to continue when you have the ability to help stop it."

"Hang on," Dakota said. "I'm a worker and I have a job to do. I follow my instructions without questioning them. That's the way of things."

"You have to choose," Doctor Prowl said. "This is your final choice. You can die here and now or you can stand against the forces that have killed innocent men, women, and children. Killing people who've done nothing but ask for the life they deserve to live."

"What have I done?" Dakota asked. "Why do I deserve to die?"

"You support the corruption," Doctor Prowl said. "You are a henchman, well henchwoman, for a diseased system. If we don't destroy you and all the Alpha Troops nothing will change. We must fight for our children and our children's children. We fight for every man, woman and child in this country who dream of peaceful and prosperous lives."

"You do realize," Dakota said. "We both have tracking systems on us. They will find us immediately and everyone with us will be killed."

"I know the systems," Doctor Prowl said. "And I know how the tracking systems work. That's why I have this case with me. If you agree to go I will remove the tracking system. You have a choice right now. Everything has been taken care of. You either come with us or you die. Which is it?"

"I will go with you," September said quickly. "I agree with what you are saying."

Dakota looked at September and wondered how she could agree so quickly to this man. Dakota knew nothing of him or if what he said was true. Dakota was so conflicted and didn't know how to continue. She thought about letting the doctor kill her so she would be out of it. It wouldn't matter who was ruling or who was oppressed. She would be dead and her problems would be over.

For a brief moment death filled Dakota's head but she knew that wasn't a path she could take. She could go with and play double agent. She would destroy the group from the inside. As her brain computed all the different options and situations that gripped her, she came to the conclusion the only option would be to truly work with them. The government was corrupt and she'd seen how low they would sink. Ever since the smuggler told her what Emperor Ross II was doing she knew change was needed.

"I'll go with you," Dakota said looking at the ground. "I cannot allow the damage to continue in our country. I will go with you."

"Good," Doctor Prowl said. "You both need to lie on the floor."

Both girls spread out on the floor while Doctor Prowl set his case down on a bed and opened all the locks, spinning the multiple tumblers to the right combinations. He opened the cover of the case and a fog poured out of it. Monte pulled out two syringes and looked them over. He very quickly injected both Dakota and September in their stomachs with the needles. Dakota felt a tingle in her stomach. At first it felt nice, warm and pleasant. In an instant, her body was wracked with pain. Dakota was struggling to see but could tell September was vomiting on the floor. Dakota vomited as her entire body started to cramp. Dakota could see Monte was shouting to the guards outside the cell but she couldn't hear what he was saying.

"I need help in here!" Doctor Prowl yelled. "We need two gurneys."

In an instant a pair of Alpha Troop women in full combat gear rushed into the room each pushing a gurney. One Alpha took Dakota, the other September. They picked them up as though they'd been sacks of grain. They placed them on the gurneys. The Alpha Troops strapped the girls onto the gurneys and pushed them down the halls. September had still been vomiting and Dakota was completely blacked out.

The Alpha Troops followed Monte as he rushed through the labyrinth substructure of the castle into an underground garage. There was an ambulance transport waiting in the garage. The Alpha Troops quickly pushed the girls into the ambulance and closed the door. Doctor Prowl was about to enter the driver's door of the transport when one of the Alpha Troop women stopped him.

"Where are you taking them?" she asked.

"The Ridge Medical Center," Doctor Prowl said. "It's the only place that can treat them. You know what these troops are, correct?"

"I've been told they are special versions of Alpha Troops," the woman scoffed. "But they don't look like much, do they?"

"They are more valuable than you could ever imagine," Doctor Prowl said. "I need to get them to the medical facility immediately. If they die Emperor Ross II will kill everyone who prevented them from getting help."

"I will alert the Emperor that the girls have been moved," the woman said.

"No," Doctor Prowl said quickly. "I will tell him. He will not be pleased and I know how to absorb his abuse. He may kill you just for delivering the news. I have to get moving though."

Doctor Prowl quickly got into the transport and took off. He tore out of the garage and onto the streets as he left the pair of Alpha Troop women looking on. The one who'd spoken to Doctor Prowl looked on in disgust.

"That didn't seem right," she said. "I'm going to alert a commander."

"I agree," the other said. "And I thought I heard something when we were talking to him, like a cover being put back in place. It came from underneath the transport."

"I thought something seemed off too," the first said.

The pair looked over where the transport had been and noticed a manhole cover. The women went to the cover and pulled it up. Beneath was another cover, steel, with steel locks they were unable to open.

Chapter #11

Nyx gave Charlie a massage as he soaked in the massive spa in a private room off his bedroom. Charlie sipped wine while Nyx worked all the tensions out of his back and shoulders when the bedroom doors flew open as Garret stormed in. Garret marched to the edge of the steaming water and looked over both rooms. He noticed how disrupted the bed sheets were. Charlie and Nyx's clothes were flung about the floor and Charlie looked content.

"God damn it!" Garret shouted. "We have massive problems Charlie. I've been trying to call you for over an hour now."

"I've been here with Nyx," Charlie said as he sipped more wine. "We've been playing."

Garret looked at Charlie with disgust. Charlie appeared half drunk and fully stoned off of sweet leaf. Charlie was wearing a black brief swimming suit and Nyx was in a white bikini. Garret could see all the fat that covered Garret's body where muscle once was. Charlie was at one time an amazing soldier and fighter but Garret doubted whether Charlie could stand in a fight any longer.

"The Beta Troops have been kidnapped again," Garret said.

"They were in the jail beneath the castle," Charlie said not caring. "They had Alpha Troops guards. There's no place that could be safer or more secure. No. You must be mistaken. They were not kidnapped."

"They were taken," Garret said. "The report I received from the Alpha Troops who were there is a doctor came to look over the Beta Troops. He called for medical gurneys to take the girls to the Ridge Medical Facility. They appeared to be very sick, vomiting, convulsing and had many other symptoms. They had to strap them down on the gurney. They took them into a parking ramp and loaded them into a waiting medical transport. The Alpha Troops questioned the doctor when he went to get into the driver's position. They spoke for a moment before he left. They noticed an opening that led into the tunnel service systems for the castle. The top cover opened easily; however, there was a locked steel cover beneath that. Sound familiar?"

"The same system they used before," Charlie said. "But if they were in the castle systems, would they have had time to get away? Could they still be there?"

"It's a labyrinth beneath there Charlie," Garret said. "We got a plasma cutter to remove the cover and sent a team of Alpha Troops down but there's little chance we'll find anything. They had this well planned out. We need to dial back the intelligence of the Beta Troops and engineer more loyalty into them. This could be disastrous."

"I wouldn't worry," Charlie said as he kissed Nyx.

"WOULDN'T WORRY?" Garret shouted. "Why the hell shouldn't we worry? This whole situation has gone to hell real damn fast."

"I still keep spies and networks out of your reach Garret," Charlie said. "No one watches me anymore. I want it that way. I want people to think I'm a strung-out drunk. I still have some tricks up my sleeve."

"Tricks?" Garret asked.

"A secret," Charlie said. "We've all heard the story. The Freedom Explorers made their last stand and had been beaten and defeated when they released the Shackle Virus. Total fabrication. It was my grandfather and his men. They'd already beaten and killed every Freedom Explorer there was. Hell, they were the ones who made the Shackle Virus in the first place."

"I had no idea," Garret said. "I can't believe this. You had me fooled Charlie. I must say, well played."

"Of course," Charlie said. "They started the rumors of the fourth lab and all that other garbage. Any rumor of the Freedom Explorers are created by my grandfather and his fighting men."

"I have a question," Nyx asked. "There was a story I've heard many times. There was a member of the Freedom Explorers who was captured and a threat was held over her that if she didn't reveal the location of the fourth lab they would harm her daughter. The rumor was she killed herself and her child but it wasn't her daughter."

"She was the last Freedom Explorer to die," Charlie said. "The story is based in reality. It happened but it wasn't the fourth lab they were trying to find. They sought information. The Freedom Explorers had discovered the virus and the plans to release it. They were trying to stop it."

"Are you serious?" Nyx interrupted to ask in a stunned state.

"History is written by the victors," Charlie said. "On an information drive is all the information related to the virus. How it works, how to create the amino acids, and how to permanently reverse it. We never found the drive. The drive is about the size of a pen. Tiny and easy to move and conceal. There's really no way to determine what really happened to it or if it even still exists. They were trying to get her to reveal the location of the drive."

"What does this have to do with the kidnapped Beta Troops?" Garret asked.

"Why did they release the virus if they'd already won?" Nyx asked.

"They released it so they could have full control of the population," Charlie said. "They blamed it on the Freedom Explorers so they looked like the hero's while they rebuilt the country. The connection with the Beta Troops is very simple. My spies have been monitoring a situation that's been developing. We believe the Freedom Explorer woman who killed herself did know where the information drive was. The location has been passed down to her granddaughter. I am allowing all of this to develop and I will smoke out the location."

"You've never been on the sweet leaf drug, have you?" Garret asked.

"Never," Charlie said. "All an elaborate sham. You two are the last I can trust explicitly. There are double agents and spies everywhere. Nyx, you are my favorite and that is true. I need you to carry out orders; very special, specific orders."

"What are those?" Nyx asked.

"You must kill all my children," Charlie said. "And the women who are pregnant with my children. There are three of them. Once they have all been confirmed dead I will marry you and we will have a child who will be heir to the throne. Can you do that?"

"I can," Nyx said, stunned by these revelations. "I'm still in shock though, I never envisioned you to be this devious. I've seen you take the sweet leaf thousands of times and you always react perfectly, even down to eye-dilation and performance enhancement."

"Hypnoligation control of my body systems," Charlie said. "A form of mind-body awareness control. I practiced for many years before I could perform convincingly. It's why I ridded myself of all other women and only kept you. It's easier to fool one person than many people. The more who saw it, the more I would have to convince."

"So how do we find the location?" Garret asked.

"My false doctor," Charlie said. "Has connections with a contact in the underground. Someone who has access to the location of the drive, if it exists. We are going to play it out to find out if the drive is real and if it is, we'll destroy it."

"Who's the doctor?" Nyx asked.

"Doctor Monte Prowl," Charlie said. "You have to know how to bend people. His little sister. He loves her like a daughter. She's the only family he has left and she's stunningly gorgeous. I had her kidnapped and taken to a pleasure house. In exchange to get her out of the pleasure house and keep her out was his loyalty to me and selling out the rebel trash that want us defeated. We got him into a group of rebels and he's been spying on them ever since. We know everything."

"Who's the person that may know the location?" Garret asked.

Nyx was glad Garret asked that question. She couldn't believe what she'd been hearing. She'd been working with this group and Doctor Prowl for some time now and she was one who had the information. Nyx couldn't believe Charlie didn't know it was her. She hoped there was some way she could get out of the castle and never return. Nyx's heart pounded as she waited for Charlie to answer the question.

"Some street walker," Charlie said. "Someone he's been playing with."

Nyx breathed a sigh of relief.

"What's the play then?" Garret asked.

"It's time to create a show of force," Charlie said. "We need to show the world we are serious."

Charlie got out of the spa and put an ornately decorated black, silk, flowing robe on. The robe hung loosely off his massive body as he tied it to cover himself up. Nyx stayed in the water as Charlie pulled out a viewer and brought up a map of North America. The map showed their empire and the five little countries that made up what was left of the old countries. He pushed a button and the map changed, showing U-Cam controlling all of North America.

"This is our play," Charlie said. "The whole of the continent. Once we control the entire continent our breathing room vastly expands. We can isolate ourselves from the world scene, or so we say. This is a play toward a much larger empire."

"You dream of a world empire?" Garret asked.

"Not in so many words," Charlie said. "But we will be the largest country by far. We will have the largest population and if this is handled right we will be feared. Other countries will line up to align with us. It will end the threat of attack. No one will dare stand against us."

"How will we accomplish this?" Garret asked.

"Very simple," Charlie said. "We are going to block off an entire city. We are going to call on all the rebels to turn themselves in. We'll put them on trial for crimes against the empire. If they refuse we'll cut the amino acid supply off to the city. We'll show them we're ready to kill millions if we are not obeyed. They will have no choice but to advocate."

"That's a dangerous course," Garret said. "If they don't turn themselves in..."

"Then we withhold the amino acid," Charlie interrupted. "We will not be bluffing. Once the people start dying in the horrible fashion the rebels will turn themselves in, nothing will stop it."

"How horrible is the death?" Nyx asked. "I've never seen anyone die that way."

"First they will feel thirsty," Charlie said. "But no amount of water will quench their thirst. Next their stomachs will churn. At first it will be like an upset stomach but within an hour or so it will feel like knives stabbing them from the inside. Fever is next, with dizziness and pain all over. Soon a person will convulse so badly they will break their back. What really kills them though is the pain. Pain in the body so great the body has no choice but to shut down completely. The entire process takes over ten hours from the first sign of symptoms."

"That's terrible," Nyx said.

"That's the point," Charlie said. "Once they see that, no one will dare question me and my rule. We will stand alone. Once we know what city they are looking at we will section off and secure that town. If we have to kill everyone and don't have the information drive we will level the city with high-heat bombings to make sure no one ever finds it. This is a good plan. Oh yes, we will have everything going our way. Once we've eliminated the city we will begin claiming our neighbors were the guilty parties. Evidence will have to be faked and payoffs granted, but it can be done. We'll take a legal position that they were trespassing and trying to steal natural resources. Then we'll move in on them with Alpha and Beta Troops."

"We have much work to do then," Garret said.

"Much of this has been taken care of," Charlie said. "I've been planning this for a long time. My first goal is to get myself into a presentable state again. I had to let myself go to fool everyone. Garret, they will all be looking at you when this starts. It will be a long time before they realize what's really going on here. Nyx, I have a report that will give you the known locations of all my children and the women who are pregnant with my children. The only one that isn't known is Alexis but I'm sure she will surface once these plans start coming together. One of my pregnant women in is the castle now. She is in the hospital ward on bed rest. She's due any day now. Go to her and kill her."

"I will," Nyx said getting out of the spa.

Nyx didn't dry off or take any cover-ups as she rushed out of the room. Charlie and Garret watched her leave before they turned back to the map.

"I'm very impressed," Garret said. "I didn't know what to do with you anymore. No one can run this country like you can."

"I was testing you," Charlie said. "Seeing if you would kill me. That's why it went so far. I had to be sure you would follow me no matter what. There was no way you would have been able to."

"Are you sure of that?" Garret said.

"I'm sure," Charlie said. "You would want to kill me with your hands out of respect of our relationship. I've been watched at all times. Had you set a finger on me you would have been dead."

"That's most likely the way I would have done it," Garret said. "This doctor, Monte Prowl, he's trustworthy?"

"Very," Charlie said. "I bent him with his sister. He knows if he double crosses us his sister is in the pleasure house. When I have a large enough lever I can move a mountain. I just need to know what the lever is and where to place it. It's all just that simple...within a year Garret, we will be rid of all our enemies and have a continental empire."

Chapter #12

In a small gym with only a few weight machines, Dakota pushed September as hard as she could. When they started with training, September could only lift about four hundred pounds on the bench press. It was a far distance from Dakota's six hundred pound lifts and an Alpha woman's eight hundred. Dakota knew with her pushing September, she would become a fighter as strong and fierce as she was.

As the pair continued their workout, Doctor Kent, Doctor Prowl, and Jerrica entered the little gym and watched them. The group knew very soon the empire would launch a revenge campaign against them for taking the Beta Troops so they had been very vigilant in the security of their work.

"Impressive," Doctor Kent said. "You two are amazing. The empire must have worked very hard to get you to this level of perfection."

"The genetic engineering," Dakota said playfully. "Only takes us so far. The rest is our own work."

"We'll need to see that work soon," Doctor Prowl said. "Our contact is working on getting the location on where the fourth lab is. Very soon we will be able to get the information we need to take down the government."

"The empire has no convictions anymore," Dakota said. "All they care about is power and pleasures. This will be an easy battle to bring them down."

"We can hope," Jerrica said.

As Jerrica was about to continue, Nyx rushed into the gym. She hadn't even taken the time to cover up since getting out of the spa with Charlie. She was in her bathing suit and shoes. Nyx was almost out of breath and was sweating heavily. Everyone was confused as to why she was there.

"Nyx," Doctor Kent said. "We weren't expecting you so soon. You really shouldn't be here, it's far too risky. What is the matter?"

"You won't believe," Nyx said panting, trying to catch her breath. "It's all been a sham. Charlie is really in control. The drugs were faked. He aspires to rule the continent. They are going to take out a city."

Nyx realized that Monte was standing in the room. She recoiled at the sight of him.

"Traitor!" Nyx screamed. "Monte has been telling Charlie everything you do here. He's working for the empire."

Everyone was dumbfounded. Jerrica looked at her big brother as he held his hands up in a submissive position.

"That's not true," Jerrica said as she looked to Dr. Prowl. "Is it?"

"Yes and no," Monte said.

"You'd best explain yourself," Doctor Kent said pulling a gun and aiming it at Monte. "And explain yourself fast."

"The empire had captured Jerrica," Monte said. "They put her in a pleasure house and were going to train her in those arts. I couldn't have my little sister there. I tried to save her but was captured. They told me we could both go free if I helped them. Charlie guaranteed me she would never have to work in one of those places again. I had no choice, but I haven't given them good or accurate information."

"It sounded pretty accurate to me," Nyx said.

"They don't know about you, do they?" Monte asked.

"No," Nyx said. "It seemed like my story was attributed to a common street walker."

"I fed him that," Monte said. "I made sure you were safe. I'm working against them. This is the best position we could be in. We are on the inside."

"Or are you really working for him and just feeding us lies?" Doctor Kent asked. "This is too fine a point to split hairs on. Monte, how can we trust you?"

"I'll give you this," Monte said. "I'll give you my word and bond. You can ask anything of me right now and I will do it for you to prove I am telling you the truth."

"You would give me," Doctor Kent said. "Jerrica's hand in marriage to prove you were on our side?"

"If that's what it took," Monte said.

"Monte!" Jerrica exclaimed. "You would give me away to him without a thought?"

"If I knew you would be safe and protected," Monte said. "Yes. It would be a good pairing. You could do far worse you know."

"It won't be necessary," Doctor Kent said. "It was a test. I believe him."

"This is all fine," Dakota said. "But what do we do now? This goes to show the levels that Charlie and the empire will go to stop you. How do we counter this kind of information attack?"

"We need to go on the offensive," Doctor Kent said. "Nyx, what is the next move for the Empire?"

"They want to rid themselves of all rebels," Nyx said. "They are going to wait and see where a rumored information drive is." Nyx quickly informed them about the real story. "Once they know the city, they will seal it off and kill the town if the rebels, all the rebels, us included, don't turn themselves in."

"How will they know when all the rebels have come forward?" Jerrica asked. "The plan doesn't make sense."

"It does when you look at the whole," Doctor Prowl said. "Once they pick a town, its fate will have been sealed. They know some rebels will turn themselves over but most won't. They are going to wipe the town out no matter what."

"So how do we stop it?" Dakota asked. "What can we do to prevent this?"

"Nyx," Doctor Prowl asked. "You said you had a location for the information drive. Did you ever find out where it was?"

"I had a friend investigate the vault," Nyx said. "It was empty. There was nothing there. She said it looked like the vault had been cleared out years ago."

"Damn it," Doctor Prowl said. "So now what do we do?"

"We steal the information," Dakota said. "We know where the amino acid comes from. All shipments are from a large factory in the milling district of Two Rivers Kansas."

"The city of falling stars," Doctor Kent said. "I don't know how many times people have attempted to breach that facility but I can tell you how many times it worked, none. Not to mention the fact that every person who's ever tried is dead."

"This could be our only shot," Jerrica said. "And we have something no one else has ever had."

"What's that?" Doctor Kent asked.

"Two Beta Troops," Jerrica said. "And a way to defeat the Alpha Troops."

"It would take a lot of careful planning," Dakota said. "But we could very easily extract information from the factory. No one can stand before us."

"How many Beta Troops are there?" Doctor Kent asked. "How many other warriors are out there who look like normal people yet kill in the blink of an eye?"

"I don't know," Dakota said. "I only know of September, Tanna and myself. I've never met another Beta Trooper. I don't know how long we were in development for."

"And you can't get any information on them at the Ridge Medical Facility?" Doctor Prowl asked.

"My information sources there are limited," Doctor Kent said. "We were lucky I was able to get what I did."

"I say we go for Two Rivers," Jerrica said. "We take down all the Alpha and send in the Betas. We'll walk right out with the formula. Once we have it they will have no choice then to deal with us."

"Deal with us could mean many things Jerrica," Doctor Kent said.

"You have no idea how cruel Charlie really is," Nyx said. "And with what he's got planned, who knows what the world will look like when he's done. If we want a country to fight for we need to act quickly."

"I'm adept at planning," September said. "Get me maps of Two Rivers. I can figure out the best way to move in on them."

"I'll try to find any information on the building and factory itself," Doctor Prowl said. "Find out what we'll be up against when we get inside."

"Keep a sharp watch though," Doctor Kent said. "We can't set off any alarms by looking at this."

Monte nodded as he left the room with Jerrica and September in step behind him. Doctor Kent, Nyx, and Dakota were left in the room alone. They waited until they were sure the others were out of hearing range before he spoke again.

"I take it there's more to what you found out?" Doctor Kent asked.

"I cannot be sure," Nyx said. "Something I feel. Charlie ordered me to kill all his children and the women who are pregnant with his children."

"Did you?" Dakota asked.

"I had an Alpha Trooper do it," Nyx said. "I got an Alpha woman to go with me. She killed the lady who was in the hospital in labor and one other who was close by. She is going after his kids now but no one knows where Alexis is."

"Alexis is in hiding for sure," Doctor Kent said. "But I would guess she would be nearby. Where is the location for the information drive?"

"Alexis has it," Nyx said. "I contacted her before I came here. She told me what she'd found. The drive is hidden in a bank vault in Two Rivers."

"Why did they put it there?" Dakota asked.

"They were being chased," Nyx said. "The empire was on to them and knew they had the information. They hid it and left the city. There was a group of them, ten I think, and they all headed different directions. The empire never knew if they'd dropped the drive in Two Rivers or if one of them took it and placed it somewhere else."

"Do we know what bank?" Doctor Kent asked.

"We do," Nyx said. "It's the empire's private bank. No commercial or civilian use, only empire business."

"That will make it slightly harder to breach," Doctor Kent said.

"How in the world did they get it in there in the first place?" Dakota asked.

"They had help on the inside," Nyx said. "Who they killed right after they placed it there so they couldn't tell anyone. It was in the final stages of the war so nobody questioned them getting killed."

"Everything that was done was so elaborate," Dakota said. "So what's our play then?"

"We will first take the bank and get the drive," Doctor Kent said. "We'll have to steal all the money and anything of value from the bank to convince them that it was a robbery. Once we have the information we'll move on the factory itself. We need to have supplies of the amino acid ready to go. We will then get our people into position to start attacking Alpha Troops and anything related to the empire. We will have to distribute the amino acid once the collapse of the government happens."

"Your troops?" Dakota asked. "I've never seen any troops around here Doctor Kent. How many people do you have?"

"We have thousands all across the country," Doctor Kent said. "But you must remember, I am a guerrilla leader so one of the first rules of fighting a guerrilla war is to always separate your troops from the commanders. The troops have no idea where we are. If they are captured they cannot reveal anything or nor can I about their locations."

"You don't know where they are?" Nyx asked.

"I don't," Doctor Kent said. "My contacts do, but I don't."

"Seems a strange setup," Nyx said.

"These are strange times we live in," Doctor Kent said. "We need to keep a sharp eye on Doctor Prowl as well. I don't know if we can trust him."

"I can get one of my girls on him," Nyx said. "She won't let us down."

"Do it now," Doctor Kent said.

Nyx took off leaving just Dakota and Doctor Kent in the room. Doctor Kent looked Dakota over. She was flushed and still sweaty from her workout. She wore clothing with the empire's emblem sewn in. Doctor Kent smiled at her.

"Are you ready for all that is about to come?" Doctor Kent asked.

"I should hope so," Dakota said. "This is what I was trained to do. I know I can perform at the levels you expect."

"Something tells me you have some doubts," Doctor Kent said.

"All my life," Dakota said. "I've believed this empire, this government, and Emperor Ross II were the right thing. I believed the empire looked out for the citizens and now I find out he's evil, corrupt, and willing to slaughter his own people to enhance his power. It's a big shift to deal with."

"What do you want to get out of your life?" Doctor Kent asked.

"For the longest time," Dakota said. "For as long as I can remember even, I wanted to be known as the best trooper in the empire. I wanted to be leading troops into battle, planning and executing covert operations. I wanted to be the emperor's go to girl whenever anything or anyone needed taking care of."

"But now you have other wishes?" Doctor Kent asked.

"Now all I long for," Dakota said. "Is to have a childhood; parents to raise me and the opportunity to experience all the things I was cheated out of by being in the Troops. I want a first kiss, a boyfriend, friends and a normal school. I want all the things I can never have."

Dakota turned away from Doctor Kent as she started to cry.

"I'll never know any of that," Dakota said. "All my life will be to serve others."

"It doesn't have to be like that," Doctor Kent said putting a hand on her shoulder. "I will give you something that will start to put things in place. It won't fix that past but it will allow you to choose your own future."

"What's that?" Dakota said turning around.

"I will let you kill Emperor Ross II," Doctor Kent said.

"What?" Dakota said turning around.

"I will guarantee you," Doctor Kent said. "That if we capture him and I'm able to get you to him in time I will have you kill him. Prime Minister Boyd too. They were the ones who took all of those dreams away from you, so you should be the one to take their futures from them."

"You would give me that honor?" Dakota asked.

"I would," Doctor Kent said.

"And in return," Dakota asked. "Shall I escort you to bed or would you want me to perform right here and now?"

"You can perform," Doctor Kent said. "Only if you want to. I give you this with no expectation of reciprocation. You are the one who should finish them."

"Thank you," Dakota said. "No one has ever been this nice to me."

"Think nothing of it," Doctor Kent said.

"Oh no," Dakota said. "I must offer something to you. Doctor Kent, anytime you want anything...I'm yours."

Chapter #13

Nyx hadn't changed yet and had been running non-stop since she'd left Doctor Kent's side. She entered the office chamber through the secret passage. She looked around but didn't see Alexis in the office. Nyx had never been more careful as she was this time in going to the house. She didn't know to what extent Charlie would go to obtain information and who was on his side. Nyx knew she had to get to Alexis and tell her what she knew.

This would be the first time ever Nyx showed up without a set meeting time. Nyx had never been so far in Alexis's secret hiding place. The exterior looked like a standard mansion with only a few people who ever came and went from it. Most of the workers entered through the school next door. Only Nyx and Alexis knew about the passage Nyx used. The other workers had their own entrance.

As Nyx paced the room, the door opened and Alexis walked in. Alexis was stunned to see Nyx standing there, but she rushed up and embraced her friend.

"Nyx," Alexis said. "What on earth are you doing here?"

"You have no idea what we're up against," Nyx said. "Charlie fooled everyone."

"What do you mean?" Alexis asked.

Alexis offered Nyx a chair and Nyx sat down. Alexis removed her sleeveless duster and sat in a chair next to Nyx. Alexis crossed her legs and leaned back in the chair, keeping her arms flat on the armrests.

"Charlie had faked the whole thing," Nyx said. "He was never hooked on drugs, never drunk. Everything was a ruse to trick us. Even Garret didn't know."

"Oh my god," Alexis said leaning forward.

Nyx really looked at Alexis for the first time since coming in. Alexis was in the outfit she always wore in the offices, the yellow top and navy tights. Sweat was beading down her body and the top was so wet it appeared to have been run under water. Alexis was in amazing shape. Her body was tone and cut. Alexis realized Nyx was studying her.

"I was working out," Alexis said. "When I saw a motion sensor go off in my office. You tripped it when you opened the door. I used a viewer to see who was here before I entered. I can never be too cautious."

"We weren't cautious enough," Nyx said. "The plans Charlie has. He made me kill all his children. I'm so sorry. I ordered an Alpha Woman to do it. She's already taken some of them out. No one knows where you are at though."

"My location has to stay secret," Alexis said.

"I may have given it away," Nyx said. "I'm so sorry."

"How?" Alexis asked.

"One of the doctors I've been working with," Nyx said. "One who's a leader of the rebels, Doctor Monte Prowl, is working with the empire. He knows I work for you. As of now it appears he's playing a double game. Charlie had taken his sister to the pleasure houses and made a deal with Doctor Prowl to keep her out. It looks like he's been giving Charlie some good and some bad information."

"We can't take the risk though," Alexis said. "There may be things he knows that he may have told. As for my siblings dying, it had to happen. I have to be the sole person in line for the empire. There were too many of them who would have ruled like our father did. I could not have allowed that to happen."

"They have the Beta Troops with them now," Nyx said. "They are with the rebels. Charlie and Garret killed a Beta Troop and that was the tipping point for her partner."

"Violence only begets violence," Alexis said. "And ruling with terror and fear will only work as long as the people are afraid of you. They are afraid of you only as long as there is something that you can take away from them. Once there's nothing left, the people have no reason to fear and you will meet a terrible end."

"Profound," Nyx said. "But what do we do?"

"Did your rebels come up with a plan for taking the information drive at Two Rivers?" Alexis asked.

"They are working on getting one together right now," Nyx said. "There was something else though, the Beta Troop knew the location for the amino acid factory. They are also working on a plan to break into the factory and gain the amino acid so they can continue with the distribution of the supply."

"I knew of the factory," Alexis said. "But it's guarded by hundreds of Alpha Troops. We've always wanted to raid it but it seemed impossible. There are other factories as well, five total that I know of, but they are guarded and secured by many different systems. There's a big secret about them."

"What's that?" Nyx asked.

"Every factory," Alexis said. "Is automated. None of the workers know the formula or even what they are working on. The people there only repair the machines and make sure they are working correctly. Shipments are guarded by Alpha Troops. There have been attempts at other locations to steal a leaving shipment but it never works. Everyone dies."

"Should I talk them out of trying to steal from the factory?" Nyx asked.

"No," Alexis said. "But they must be very careful. They must have plenty of their weapons that can take down the Alpha Troops. By the time we are done we must wipe all the Alpha Troops out."

"What about the Beta Troops?" Nyx asked. "They seem far more deadly and dangerous than the Alpha Troops."

"We don't need to worry about them yet," Alexis said. "Father will learn technology is a double edged sword that cannot be wielded by the untrained. He should have stopped with the Alpha Troops."

"What do you mean?" Nyx asked.

"That is my little secret for now," Alexis said. "Nyx, our prime goal is to keep both of us safe and keep the information flowing."

"I came here with a goal in mind though," Nyx said. "I need a girl to watch Doctor Monte Prowl. He told us he was feeding misinformation to Charlie and Garret and said he didn't tell them about me or that I know you. There may be some truth to that but they threatened his little sister so there's no telling what he is truly willing to do."

"I know someone who'll work perfect," Alexis said as she moved to a network device and typed in a message. "Charlie never suspected when I joined these schools that I would begin teaching espionage and counter-espionage. What better source of talent. Those girls' abilities are beyond measure. They are the largest information network in the world. They feed everything they get back to me. Charlie will never know how we defeated him. Control the information and you control the direction they head."

"What about you though?" Nyx asked. "It's reasonable to estimate that someone's been watching me. They've seen me going into that mansion next door. Do you think they would search out the areas around it?"

"It is possible," Alexis said. "I believe that it's time we abandon this place. You and I will go to Two Rivers and gather reconnaissance. We will take the best girls with us. I will send a report to my dear father. In your attempt to kill me I captured you and am holding you hostage. I'm betting his plan included marrying you and you having his heir?"

"How did you know?" Nyx asked.

"If he had you kill the other children," Alexis said. "It was a rather easy judgment he would want you to bear the heir. I will hold you hostage and we will produce a doctor's report that says you are carrying his child. He will be forced to deal with us."

"They are planning to destroy a large town though," Nyx said. "Withhold the amino acid."

"Then we have to make sure they come to Two Rivers," Alexis said. "We'll have the amino acid in our possession so we can distribute it. No one has to die Nyx. We will wait though, long enough to have full reports on what is developing, before we send my father the reports."

"When will we leave this place?" Nyx asked.

"Tonight," Alexis said. "I already alerted my girls on what to do. We will sneak out under cover of darkness and make our way to Two Rivers."

"I left the castle without any clothing," Nyx said. "Do you have any garments that would fit me?"

"I do," Alexis said.

Alexis stood and walked to a tall closet door. She opened the doors to reveal a number of various outfits hanging in the closet. She handed Nyx a pair of navy tights and a yellow top. Nyx put the garments on over her suit. The tights only went halfway down her calves and the top was tight and clingy, exposing the whole of her arms and not touching the top of the tights.

"Sorry," Alexis said. "I don't have anything that would fit better."

"This works fine," Nyx said. "I'm finally in colors that mean something."

Alexis smiled and was about to say something when a buzzer went off in the room. Alexis's face flushed and she looked at a viewer and gasped with horror. Nyx looked at the viewer and saw Alpha Troops were rushing into the house. They had broken down the front door and were killing the women and men who were in the hallways of the house.

"How did they find this place?" Alexis asked.

"Oh my god," Nyx said. "I thought Charlie was acting out of sorts. He offered me a gift before we started tonight, this suit. He must have placed a tracker in it. Damn it, how could I have been so stupid not to think of that. I have to get out of it."

"Not so fast," Alexis said stopping Nyx as she was starting to take her top off. "We can use that. What better way to make sure they end up in Two Rivers than if your suit is in Two Rivers?"

Alexis grabbed some under garments out of the closet and tossed them to Nyx.

"Change," Alexis said. "Quickly. But we keep the suit with us."

Nyx followed the order and quickly stripped down. She put the new garments on before putting the top and tights back on. Alexis put the suit in a small bag before putting her sleeveless duster back on.

"How are we going to get out of here?" Nyx asked. "They'll see us leaving the house next door."

"We are not going that way," Alexis said. "Follow me."

Alexis grabbed a key and opened the bottom drawer of a large file cabinet. The drawer was full of papers and folders. Alexis pushed them far back and Nyx saw a hole under the file cabinet. It was barely big enough for the small girls to squeeze though.

"Slip in there," Alexis said as a pounding was heard on the door. "Quickly. There's a platform to stand on. Wait for me when you reach it."

Nyx obeyed and quickly struggled to slip into the hole. It was barely big enough and she had to compress her chest to slide it though. Nyx felt the platform in the darkened chamber that she stood in. Alexis had an easier time coming through the hole. When she was on the platform next to Nyx, Alexis moved the folder back into position before closing and locking the file cabinet. The room was now pitch dark. Nyx felt Alexis grab her hand and pull her to the left.

Nyx slowly walked behind Alexis. She held her hand in the pitch blackness the entire way. Nyx realized they were on a metal spiral staircase descending down into the ground. She heard water rushing below them. The staircase ended and they stood on a slick rough surface. The air was heavy with moisture as Alexis continued to lead Nyx in the darkness. Nyx felt they were walking along a rock wall when Alexis turned on her flashlight.

They were in a cavern about twenty feet high with a ten foot river of water rushing alongside of them. There was no ledge on the other side of the river. Alexis waited for a moment as around the bend a water transport arrived. The girls quickly jumped on. The transport had no lights on. Nyx couldn't tell anything about the craft except from the quick flashes of light that Alexis had given with her flashlight. The pilot was a woman who was dressed the same as them and wearing night-vision goggles. The craft was bare and moved silently through the water with precision controls.

"This will get us to safety," Alexis said. "From there I have jets waiting that will get us to Two Rivers. Before we board the jet we will put the suit in a box and block any satellite from picking up the signal. It will disappear on them and reappear in Two Rivers."

"Do you have a hideout there?" Nyx asked.

"I do," Alexis said. "And for every surprise they have for us, we will have three for them."

Chapter #14

Sweat poured down Charlie's face and body as the weight machine offered more resistance to his muscles. Since Charlie had revealed his plan to the two in his inner circle he was determined to get himself back into shape. It was the first day of his goal and he realized just how far he'd let himself slip. Charlie had attempted to lift the 250 pounds he used to be able to lift but it was too much for him. Charlie used a lighter amount, 125 pounds, and had already set up a six month plan to get him back into shape.

As Charlie concentrated on pushing the weights up, Garret marched into the room. He was flanked by two female Alpha Troop guards in the black combat gear minus the helmets. Both women towered over Garret and Charlie. They were carrying large assault rifles and had a pistol and knives in the belts around their waists. Garret watched Charlie lift for a moment before speaking.

"I've received some report Emperor Ross II," Garret said.

Charlie quickly finished his set and stood up as he looked over to Garret and the women.

"Thank you Prime Minister Boyd," Charlie said with a smile. "Things have gotten sloppy around here and it's high time we made sure protocols are being followed."

"I agree," Garret nodded.

"Then why are these women not in proper uniform?" Charlie asked.

"What do you mean?" Garret said.

"They are to be in helmets at all times," Charlie said. "With their heads exposed the group of terrorists could kill them. They need to have strict discipline at all times."

Garret turned to the women.

"Get helmets now," Garret barked. "Then return and post outside this door."

"Stop," Charlie said. "Both of you, on your knees."

The Alpha Troopers looked at each other before obeying the command. Both women dropped to their knees which put their heads slightly below Charlie. Charlie looked at the women with disgust before picking up a ten-pound dumbbell with his right hand.

"I'll give you a warning right now," Charlie said as he moved directly in front of one of the Alpha Troops and stared her down. "There's no room for slack, no room for disobedience. Tell all the Alpha Troops the orders and laws need to be followed by the letter and any dissention away from those rules will be viewed as treason against the empire."

"We will," the trooper said.

"Goddamn right you will!" Charlie yelled.

Charlie pulled his right arm back and swung with everything he had, hitting the Alpha Trooper in the jaw with the dumbbell. She was stunned and fell back bracing herself against the wall, spitting blood from her mouth. Charlie did the same thing to the other woman. She fell to the ground in a pile but quickly picked herself and moved to a position of attention. A look of rage came over his face and he slammed the dumbbell into the second Alpha Trooper's face. He continued until she fell over onto her back. Charlie laughed.

"Tell them death will be waiting for anyone who breaks protocol," Charlie said. "Go now and when you come back, you are to guard this room from inside."

The Alpha Troops quickly scrambled out of the room as Garret and Charlie looked on. Garret looked over Charlie who still had rage in his eyes and was pleased. He realized things would be taken care of.

"What are your reports?" Charlie asked as he returned to the weight machine.

"The first one is sensitive," Garret said. "Nyx had an Alpha Trooper kill your children. We've confirmed they are almost all dead."

"She didn't do it herself?" Charlie asked.

"None of them," Garret said.

"You said almost all are dead," Charlie said.

"She never found Alexis," Garret said.

"She's hidden well," Charlie said.

"There's more to the report though," Garret said. "This might be difficult to hear."

"That Nyx escaped Falling Ridge with Alexis," Charlie said.

"How did you know?" Garret stuttered.

"I told you I had a vast spy network," Charlie said. "You didn't really believe I could be sleeping with the enemy, did you?"

"I didn't know she was the enemy," Garret said dumbfounded. "I suspected but never confirmed. So was so cautious with her actions, never gave anything away."

"The oldest trick in the book," Charlie said. "The emperor plays dumb. Everyone thinks all he cares about is pleasure. Everyone had their eyes on you when I began developing the spy network. I made sure I could get a girl with a rough background. Someone who could be turned very easily. She's monitored every word you and I have ever said to each other. Why do you think I told her I wanted to marry her, have her bear my heir? It was all to build trust. I said you two were the only ones I trusted and it's true. She did exactly what I thought she would."

"But she escaped with Alexis," Garret protested.

"That's what we want," Charlie said. "They will run. I'm sure the city they run to will be the one with the information drive. I gave Nyx the gift of a bathing suit before we entered the spa, which is why we were wearing gear in the spa, normally we were nude. There is a tracker in it. The suit led us directly to Alexis. Nyx was being so careful not to be watched. That was the confirming giveaway; someone with nothing to hide wouldn't be so careful."

"You're tracking the suit then," Garret said. "It will tell us what city to go to?"

"It will," Charlie said. "We will know exactly where they are. I set it up the same day. I revealed everything the way I did so Nyx would run and not take the time to change clothes. I've studied her actions enough to know how she responds to crisis."

"This is incredible," Garret said. "I had no idea. You played this part so perfectly."

"I did," Charlie said.

Charlie was about to speak when the door opened and the two Alpha Troops returned to the room with their helmets on and took up posts on either side of the door. Charlie and Garret smiled. Charlie got up from the machine, dried his face with a towel, and tossed the towel on the machine.

"Follow me," Charlie said. "All of you. We have more work to do."

Charlie led the way, with Garret beside him and the Alpha Troops a step behind. Anytime they arrived to a door, Charlie made one of the Alpha Troopers open the door and the other go in first and make sure there was no danger. They walked from one side of the palace to the other and went up a floor. They made their way to a room and Charlie opened the door and swaggered into the room.

The room was a fancy bedroom, colored in deep, rich reds and browns. A massive four post bed was in the center of the room with stunning draperies and tapestries on the walls. The bed was covered with silk and satin sheets, red with grey and brown patterns throughout. The sheets were pulled up to the waist of Adam Plains, who looked very content, sweaty and dehydrated.

Sitting above the sheets on either side were two gorgeous women. Both looked to be around twenty years old with tanned skin and long dark hair. They were curvy and very voluptuous. Both women had pouty lips drawn into massive smiles. The woman on the right was wearing a party costume. The costume was brightly colored but didn't cover very much of her body. The woman on the left was in a traditional, elegant rose colored dress which was haltered and short.

"Meet Adam Plains," Emperor Ross II said. "He was saved by Doctor Monte Prowl."

"Saved?" Prime Minister Boyd asked.

"Adam was a brilliant mind at the Ridge Medical Facility," Emperor Ross II said. "Before he fell to drugs and women. He failed out of the school, but Doctor Prowl found him and saved him. He nursed him back to health. Well, his little sister Jerrica did most of that at the Doctor's request. Doctor

Prowl secretly hoped Adam would marry Jerrica and be her protector."

"Why is he here now though?" Prime Minister Boyd asked.

"Insurance," Emperor Ross II said. "I have a feeling Doctor Prowl is going to try and play both hands. He will appear to be loyal to us and give us information. He will give us some useful information and also some lies. He will continue his work with the rebel group he helped found. That way, no matter which side wins, he will have a home to run to."

"Snake," Prime Minister Boyd said. "We should kill him now."

"No, no, no," Emperor Ross II said. "We must use him. Now that we have Adam here we can verify the information he gives us."

Garret looked over the man on the bed. His arms were thin yet well defined. His droopy mustache seemed to flop over his thin, pale lips. He hadn't taken his attention off the pair of women who were in the bed with him. The women were all over the man. They kept their hands on him in just the right way so the man couldn't forget they were there to please him and only him. Garret wasn't sure of this plan but was interested to see where it would play out.

"What broke him?" Prime Minister Boyd asked. "Was it just the women, or did you re-hook him on sweet leaf?"

"Just the women," Emperor Ross II said. "He had been so lonely and unable to find a woman on his own. He was tormented by Jerrica Prowl, who had been so hot and cold toward him. All he wanted was someone to have fun with. We can provide that."

"So what's our play then?" Prime Minister Boyd asked. "Once we have the location what are we going to do?"

"Adam," Emperor Ross II almost shouted. "Tell us all your groups' plans."

"We have troops," Adam said. "We are working on finding a cure for the Shackle Virus. That is our prime goal so you can't bend the country with death."

"We knew that," Emperor Ross II said. "What about the ability to kill Alpha Troops?"

"Our compound," Adam said not taking his eyes off the women. "Thickens their blood so it can't flow as fast, slowing all aspects of their body and making their heart work much harder."

"Interesting ploy," Emperor Ross II said. "Is there any way we can counter it? Something we can give the Alpha Troops so they are resistant to this?"

"We've never looked into that," Adam said. "We had no desires to save any of them. The group has a lot of the compound ready to go. If the Alphas are hit by two or three of those tainted darts it will thicken the blood to the point of death. We had enough to take out just about every Alpha Troop you've made."

"If two darts would kill them," Prime Minister Boyd asked. "Why did they use only one and then shoot them?"

"Confusion," Adam said. "The first time we shot them was to create confusion. You wouldn't have learned about the darts if you didn't have someone in the group. So it was done to create conflicting reports and just be annoying."

"They've done their homework," Prime Minister Boyd said. "Do they really think they can take us down? Do they really believe they stand a chance against the empire?"

"They are already planning how they will start the new government," Adam said.

"And my daughter is with them?" Emperor Ross II asked. "They are helping Alexis?"

"They are," Adam said. "She has lots of plans on how the country will look once you are gone. There were a lot of people who seemed to be willing to join up with us."

"Do you think they can have success?" Prime Minister Boyd asked.

"They are well organized," Adam said. "And have the ability to move about with you knowing. You've seen what we can do. They are ready to move on the empire."

"Very well," Emperor Ross II said. "Adam, thank you for your help. Is there anything else I can get you?"

"How about one of those guards?" Adam asked. "Those ladies look like they could have some fun with us."

"He's a man of good taste," Emperor Ross II said. "Guards, remove your helmets, belts and boots. Join them in the bed."

The Alpha Troop women followed the order instantly. They removed the items and placed them in a pile on the floor. The women looked unsure of what they were about to do but they slowly joined Adam and the other women in the bed. Adam quickly started kissing both of them while the other girls smiled and joined in.

"Everything to your liking?" Emperor Ross II asked.

"Very much so," Adam said. "Yes."

"Good," Emperor Ross II said. "Alpha Troops, kill him."

Within the blink of an eye, before Adam could even register what Emperor Ross II had said, the Alpha Troop women had their arms around his neck and twisted in one motion, breaking his neck. Adam fell limp in the bed while the other women who were with him recoiled in horror. Emperor Ross II simply smiled as the Alpha Women put their gear back on.

"What was that for?" Prime Minister Boyd asked. "We could have used him."

"Not anymore," Emperor Ross II said. "Now is the time we take back control. Come, there's much work to be done."

Chapter #15

Set on the bank of a large river on the east side, the bank of a man-made channel on the west side, Two Rivers was a modern engineering marvel, completely contemporary, a merger of many cities that had been destroyed during the wars, was a massive hub for transportation and distribution set in the center of the country. Although the city itself was no more than fifty years old, parts of Two Rivers looked decrepit, derelict and destroyed. It was a stark contrast to the main corridor of the city that seemed to have been rebuilt every few years so it remained fresh and vibrant.

The main corridor was the area surrounding the two main roads going through Two Rivers and was a popular destination for many travelers. The corridor was full of theaters, museums, sporting arenas, pleasure houses and educational facilities. The two roads that created the main corridor were the only roads that had bridges going over the rivers that made up the boarders of the city, making them very heavily traveled roads, the only ways in and out of Two Rivers.

Near the northern most tip of Two Rivers sat an industrial compound. The compound was massive and sprawling. A large, square brick building sat in the center with many smaller outbuildings. Six tall smokestacks spewed thick black smoke. A ten foot, reinforced brick fence surrounded the compound, which made it impossible to look onto the compound's courtyard and buildings from the nearby road. Only one gate granted entry and exit, but it was electrified and had a pair of Alpha Troops inside and outside, and a pair more of Troops in a guard shack, a concrete structure attached to the fence that housed all the video monitoring equipment for the grounds.

The compound was being investigated through a pair of binoculars from a tall building three blocks to the south. On the roof of the building, Doctor Kent and Jerrica had breached security by posing as a repair crew. They were gathering information for the coming battle. Within the wall they saw transport trucks shuffling product around. The trucks were controlled by satellites and had no drivers. The building itself had no windows, only one walk in door and one truck door. There were Alpha Troops everywhere within the compound.

"There has to be at least twenty Alpha Troops inside that fence," Doctor Kent said. "This is going to be very difficult but I think we can take most of them out from this vantage."

"I don't know," Jerrica said looking on. "If there are troops against the walls there will be no way to hit them. Who knows, plus there are no good posting sites to the north. We'd have to rely on one sniper location."

"Once the troops start dying," Doctor Kent said. "There will be mass confusion. Any troops in the courtyard will either rush toward the building or the guard shack. We will be able to get them. Once we have a majority of them down we can storm the gate. With the Beta Troops on our side, the remaining Alpha Troops won't stand a chance."

"You hope," Jerrica said.

"Hope what?" Doctor Kent asked.

"That that's how they respond," Jerrica replied. "I would feel much better if we had a second watch."

"We'll work on something," Doctor Kent said.

Doctor Kent was about to continue when Dakota and September entered through the roof. They approached the Doctor and Jerrica and Dakota passed a note to the Doctor. Doctor Kent looked the note over and then looked to Dakota and September, who were both disguised as street walkers. He handed the note to Jerrica who looked it over with a raised eyebrow.

"You're sure this is accurate?" Jerrica asked.

"Positive," Dakota said. "I used certain talents to obtain this."

"You didn't need to go that far," Doctor Kent said.

"I killed four Alpha Troops," Dakota said. "September killed two. There's no doubt about it, Emperor Ross II knows where we are at."

"We've been here for a week," Doctor Kent said. "I was wondering if our plan would work. This confirms that Nyx and Alexis have set off the tracker Nyx had on her. Alpha Troops are on the move. We visually confirmed Alpha Troops were setting up road blocks on the four bridges that enter and exit the city. A damn to the north is being opened while one to the south is closing. They are raising the level of the rivers to make sure no one can leave using that outlet. With those four bridges, they can keep this city completely closed off."

"I know they are corrupt," September said. "But to kill a population of over four million people? How in the world does Emperor Ross II think he can get away with this? Surely there will be peace-keeping missions that learn of what happens here. The international community won't stand for this."

"What can they do?" Jerrica asked. "They will be stopped now by the factor that's always stopped them, the Shackle Virus. No one dares to stop the Ross Empire because they know a spy could carry the Shackle Virus to their country and release it. They would have to be dependent on U-Cam for help. It's the same reason they will not help us."

"Once we've breached this compound," Doctor Kent said. "And broken into the bank there will be no reason to fear them. Any word on the plan for extracting the information drive from the bank?"

"We have located the bank," Dakota said. "And are working on a plan to get the drive out."

"I don't understand how it could stay hidden though," Jerrica said. "Wouldn't they have to pay for a deposit box? Couldn't that be tracked?"

"That's the beauty of how it was hidden," Dakota said. "From the information that was received, the drive was in the vault, hidden inside the baseboards of the wall. From the description it sounds as if there was no way anyone would have ever been able to notice where it was."

"How much money do they estimate is in the bank?" Doctor Kent asked.

"From the reports I've seen," Dakota said. "I would estimate at least ten million dollars in cash and cash equivalents."

"Seems like a very low amount," Doctor Kent said. "For such a secure bank."

"We may have a different problem," Jerrica said looking into a communicator. "All of the hospitals that administer the shots have just been locked."

"What?" Doctor Kent asked.

"The hospitals are locked," Jerrica said. "They are cutting the supply of the amino acid off. They are getting ready to kill Two Rivers. I can't believe they would move this quickly."

"They know we're here," Doctor Kent said.

"How long before people start dying?" September asked.

"It will take around sixty hours," Doctor Kent said. "Before the first signs of symptoms appear."

"Where's Doctor Prowl?" Dakota asked.

"He's with Emperor Ross II," Doctor Kent said. "The emperor and the prime minister were flying in this morning. They'd had a command post set up and were going to stay there. I don't know where it's at yet. Nyx was going to find out."

"Why hasn't anyone received a report on Adam yet?" Dakota asked. "There's something wrong there. Adam hasn't been seen or heard from in a week."

"I know," Doctor Kent said. "I don't even want to venture a guess about what has happened to him, but I can approximate. He most likely ran into the emperor's troops. If there have been no reports, and neither Nyx nor Alexis can garner anything, we can only assume he's dead. If he's alive, we will find him. We need to move up our plans though. We must make contact with Nyx and let them know that the bank plan will need to be pushed up to tonight."

"Tonight?" Dakota, September, and Jerrica said in unison.

"We can't push it that far forward," Dakota said.

"If all the troops inside are Alpha," Doctor Kent said. "Then we'll just have to kill them. Dakota and September, your intelligence will be needed in getting through the vault. You will have to breach it."

"I've never done anything like that before," Dakota said. "I wouldn't know where to begin. There are so many different ways they could have locked the vault. I wouldn't know where to start."

"By the time we get there I'm sure something will come to you," Doctor Kent said.

"Something's happening," Jerrica said as she looked toward the compound.

They all turned and saw a large cargo transport vehicle pulling up to the gates. The transport stopped at the gates and the driver exited. An Alpha Troop took controls of the vehicle, opened the gate, and drove directly to the cargo door on the compound. The transport unhooked from the trailer it was pulling, backed into the cargo door, and within a minute was pulling a trailer out of the compound.

When the transport was out of the gate and the gate had been closed, the Alpha Troop and the driver switched positions. The transport, being escorted by two vehicles containing four Alpha Troops each, one in the front the other behind, turned down a narrow street. The trailer in the yard was hooked to a smaller yard vehicle and was pulled into the building. When all the vehicles had stopped moving, the Alpha Troop guards returned to their original positions.

"Interesting," Doctor Kent said. "They never allow the amino acid to be away from Alpha Troops."

"I couldn't tell," Dakota said. "How many people were in that truck, but there was more than just the driver."

"There could also be more in the cargo hold," Doctor Kent said. "We have to assume there are as many Alpha Troops on the transport as it can hold."

"They said the building was all automated," Dakota said. "But how many people do you think will be inside?"

"Once again," Doctor Kent said. "As many as they can get. I'm sure this has to be one of the most protected buildings in the country. The only thing that would have more guards would be the castle itself."

"We move on the bank tonight," Jerrica said. "Do you think our location will be secure enough to make sure we're not discovered?"

"I believe security should be adequate," Doctor Kent said. "And Doctor Prowl will not know the location. There's too much at risk. He must be kept in the dark on the fact we are moving the operation to tonight."

"He won't know about it," Jerrica said. "I can't believe he'd turn his back on me though. I want this freedom for the people of the country."

"The threats they hold over him can cause any man to do strange things," Doctor Kent said.

"Do you have a sister?" Jerrica asked.

"I'm an only child," Doctor Kent said. "But I know how strong family can be bound together. I've seen it before. The emperor knows Monte will do anything for you Jerrica. We need to keep you protected too. I think it would be best if you spent your time with the Beta Troops."

"Really?" Jerrica asked.

"I believe so," Doctor Kent said. "We cannot take the risk of you being captured. If the Empire gets you, there is no telling what they will force Monte to do."

"As Monte protects me," Jerrica said. "I must protect him."

"You can keep her safe, right?" Doctor Kent asked turning to Dakota. "You will protect Jerrica with everything you have?"

"They would have to kill us both," Dakota said.

"Very good," Doctor Kent said. "It's time we move out. We need to rest up and review the final plans. Tonight we can have no errors when we take the bank."

"Do you think we can actually break into it?" Jerrica asked. "And get out alive?"

"We have no other choice," Doctor Kent said. "It's time the emperor knows how much we despise him."

Chapter #16

The minor castle had been built to resemble the great castle that dotted the European villages of ancient times. It looked out of place against the futuristic mansions that were closely set together on the east side of the City of Falling Stars. The east side of Two Rivers was flush with money. It was one of the nicest neighborhoods in the entire country. The opulent mansions were surrounded by lavish landscaping and ornately decorated trees stood near the main corridor of the city. It was evident where the wealth really sat.

The castle was made of light colored granite and stood slightly taller than all of the mansions. It had a grass green hedge that blocked the view from outside to in, which had been reinforced with stone and Alpha Troops. Everywhere on the grounds of the castle, Alpha Troops swarmed and stood vigilant. The roof tops and spires of the castle glinted in the sunlight from the Alpha Troops that stood above with their guns at the ready. The entrances had allowed only two transports to enter in the previous week. They were both utilitarian and bulletproof military transports that carried three special people.

From the top of one of the spires, Emperor Ross II, Prime Minister Boyd and Doctor Monte Prowl looked out over the city. From the spire they saw the nearby wealth and power. They looked upon the distant poverty and oppression. They could see Alpha Troops in the distance, setting up road blocks over the bridges that would take people out of the city. Within the city, they saw the massive amount of Alpha Troops patrolling the city. They knew, as did all the citizens of the City of Falling Stars, the entire city would be in lockdown very soon.

"All Alpha Troop divisions are in place," Prime Minister Boyd said. "We are ready to seal the city on your orders Emperor."

"Good," Emperor Ross II said. "This will be perfect. We will show the world what we can do. I requested you both to discuss the reports I received."

"Reports?" Prime Minister Boyd asked. "What reports do you have that haven't crossed my eyes?"

"There are two," Emperor Ross II said. "The first is that Nyx was attempting to kill Alexis when Nyx was captured by my daughter. Alexis is holding Nyx captive in a compound here in Two Rivers."

"That makes no sense," Prime Minister Boyd said. "We know Nyx and Alexis are working together. We know they are planning together. This is a false report."

"That's what I assumed," Emperor Ross II said. "But here's the question, we know the tracker was set off here in Two Rivers, so are they here or did they send the suit with the tracker here?"

"I haven't heard either way where they are at," Doctor Prowl said. "They haven't sent any communications to my contacts for at least a week now."

"If they know what we have planned," Prime Minister Boyd said. "We can bet they would be far away from here...what is the second part of the report?"

"I wouldn't brush them off so quickly Prime Minister," Doctor Prowl said. "They are devious and want revenge. They seek to rid the country of the empire. There is a good chance they are here."

"Have any of the cameras or satellites received confirmation they are here?" Prime Minister Boyd asked.

"No," Emperor Ross II said. "I've got all our spies on it right now. If they are here we will find them."

"What is the second part of the report then?" Prime Minister Boyd asked.

"That Nyx is pregnant with my child," Emperor Ross II said.

There was a stunned silence. Garret knew the emperor wanted an heir that followed his ideas of how U-Cam should be governed. Charlie was looking out over the city. He didn't speak a word or look at either of the men who stood on the rooftop with him. Prime Minister Boyd knew this information would greatly affect how Charlie made decisions.

"What is there to substantiate this report?" Prime Minister Boyd asked.

"Two doctor's reports have confirmed the pregnancy," Emperor Ross II said. "And a note from Nyx herself. She swore she was going to tell me when we were in the spa, but you interrupted us. She isn't very far along and wants protection. She is afraid Alexis will use her as a bargaining chip and force me to give power to my daughter in exchange for saving her life and the life of my child."

"And all your other children are dead?" Prime Minister Boyd asked.

"All but Alexis," Emperor Ross II said. "Nyx had an Alpha Troop kill the rest. Doctor Prowl, in your professional medical opinion, do you think Nyx is expecting?"

"I'd need to see the medical records," Doctor Prowl said.

Charlie handed Monte a folder full of medical reports. Doctor Prowl looked the documents over and peered over every little nuance. He looked for any clue indicating the information contained within wasn't the truth. After reading every document, Doctor Prowl took a deep breath.

"All the paperwork is legit," Doctor Prowl said. "Looking this over, I would say she is pregnant. One issue though, these pictures and blood work reports that confirm the pregnancy could be from a different woman. It would be very easy to put Nyx's name on a different report. These doctors could have been bought."

"So you can't confirm or deny it?" Emperor Ross II asked.

"I can't," Doctor Prowl said. "Not without examining Nyx herself."

"Damn it," Emperor Ross said.

"What's the issue?" Prime Minister Boyd said. "It's fake."

"I'm sorry Prime Minister," Emperor Ross II said. "I can't take that chance. I have a plan"

"What?" Prime Minister Boyd asked.

"I have to know for sure," Emperor Ross II said. "I'm putting out an order, Nyx is to be found and delivered to me, unharmed. Woe to the person who hurts her."

"Sir?" Prime Minister Boyd asked.

"I will have a doctor look her over immediately," Emperor Ross II said. "If she's pregnant, she will bear the child, if not, I will kill her with my own hands."

"If she's not pregnant," Doctor Prowl asked. "Who will bear your heir?"

"I will use a Beta Troop," Emperor Ross II said. "They are genetically better than an average person. My heir would be better, superior. That is the course of action we shall take."

"If she is pregnant, why would you want to keep the child?" Prime Minister Boyd asked. "You just had her kill your other children. Let's kill her and be done with it."

"If she's pregnant I have special plans for the child," Charlie said. "A girl will be put in the pleasure houses, a boy will be kill in front of his mother. The world needs to see what happens if I am defied. I will show everyone that my law is the only law."

"What about in the near term?" Prime Minister Boyd asked. "What are we going to do here in Two Rivers?"

"Seal the city," Emperor Ross II said. "Seal it now. Anyone attempting to cross the barricades is to be shot on site. No mercy. Once the city is sealed, round up some of the people, anyone who's out in the streets. Gather them in a single location. Find a boy, someone innocent. Tell the world we want all the rebels to turn themselves in or all these people will die. Have the boy tell the world the rebels are destroying the city and causing the emperor to withhold the amino acid. He will tell the world we don't want to destroy these people, but we must smoke out the rebels. Say we've discovered plots against us and these are the consequences of those plots. We know the people who are behind the plots are here in the City of Falling Stars right now. Tell them we will spare the entire city and allow the traitors to be tried in international courts."

"What?" Doctor Prowl asked.

"We are extending them every courtesy," Emperor Ross II said. "We must make this as legal as possible. We must be careful so the international commissions cannot send investigators here to file reports."

"They wouldn't dare send investigators here," Prime Minister Boyd said. "They've never asked to before."

"Times are changing," Emperor Ross II said. "Remember the larger plan, if they think or even suspect what our true motives are, the international community will be outraged. They cannot know the plan until the very end. They cannot know until the endgame has been set in motion."

"Even still," Prime Minister Boyd said. "They can be bought, bullied, or eliminated easily enough."

"We can't overextend our hand," Emperor Ross II said. "Not yet. All moves from here on out must be played with caution. I want a video out first thing in the morning with all the news wires around the world showing the boy beg for his life. It will be very powerful. The most powerful, emotional video ever sent over the wire. We will have victory like no one would ever believe."

"How do we handle any plans the rebels have?" Prime Minister Boyd asked

"Doctor Prowl," Emperor Ross II said. "Go to your contacts. Stay with them from here on out and report back to us all the dealings they do. I want to know exactly where they are. We will wipe them out in the morning. There can be no mistakes. We have to destroy anyone who knows too much."

"And the Beta Troops?" Prime Minister Boyd asked. "How do we get them back?"

"We shall soon have more," Emperor Ross II said. "Those two can be sacrificed for the coming of our new country. It is time. Prime Minister Boyd, send the communication and seal off the city."

Prime Minister Boyd tried to swallow in a throat suddenly dry. He knew all along this order would take place but he couldn't have prepared himself for the magnitude of what he was about to do. Garret slowly pulled his communicator out of his pocket and entered his activation code. He paused before he sent the prearranged message to all the Alpha Troops.

The men looked out over the city. The sun had begun to set and appeared ever closer to the western horizon. Through the binoculars they saw the panic set in near the barricades. The Alpha Troops had closed the roads which stranded hundreds of cars that were in the process of leaving the city for any number of reasons, sealing the fate of every person inside.

The people at the bridges exited their cars and yelled at the troops. The Alpha Troops could only tell them they were following orders and the people were to get back into their cars and return to their homes or places of business. The people quickly grew agitated. Panic and confusion quickly led to chaos.

At all four bridges, people left their cars and walked to the barricades to demand answers that would never come. The Alpha Troops held their ground and warned the people to return to their cars and go home. No matter what the people did, nothing persuaded the Alpha Troops to answer their questions or allow them to leave.

It happened at the northern most bridge first, where people from the financial district were on the bridge. They were on their way home from work in Two Rivers to where they lived in Nicolette, a small but affluent town ten miles to the north. One of the men on the bridge didn't want to wait. He could tell the arguing was getting nowhere so he went to his vehicle and tried to ram past the blockade. He was met with heavy gunfire.

The Alpha Troops wasted no time in opening fire at all locations. They killed everyone who had still been sitting on the bridges. When the guns had stopped, thousands of bodies were lifeless on the roadway. The Alpha Troops returned to their guard positions. They were even safer since there were massive amounts of driverless cars blocking the way to the barricades.

From the spire of the castle, Charlie watched with a sick smile on his face. Even Prime Minister Boyd had second thoughts about what had just happened. The death toll from this night was going to be catastrophic and he knew nothing could prevent it.

"The roads are sealed," Garret said looking into his communicator. "No one can get in or out. All standard communication channels are blocked. We control the information going in and coming out."

"Perfect," Charlie said. "Move them to phase two."

"Phase two initiated," Garret said as he entered codes into his communicator.

They watched from the spire as more Alpha Troops came into view from buildings and transports. The Alpha Troops were heavily armed and wasted no time in capturing any person on the streets. No one was spared. The troops grabbed people and took them in transports to a small sports arena that had already been converted into a detention center. Within five minutes, the streets which had been full of people were now void of any life other than Alpha Troopers.

The tasteless smile on Charlie's face got bigger as more people disappeared into the transports. Everything had gone exactly as he'd planned. He knew after that night everyone would fear their emperor, who they had previously thought was a joke.

Chapter #17

The sun had begun to set as a transport raced down the city streets of Two Rivers. The jet black transport weaved between other vehicles. It drove quickly and did not stop for red lights. People on the streets watched as the transport, with blacked out windows, burned out around corners. The vehicle pulled up to a building and slammed to a stop in front of the door.

The building was red brick, with tinted windows. It was only two stories and looked strange set between all the modern skyscrapers and taller buildings in the area. The building had a planter box that contained green shrubs beneath the windows. A single door was reinforced with steel rods and had already been locked for the evening. Figures were seen behind the door, shadows, barely visible through the darkened glass.

The vehicle stopped and stayed running. It waited as Alpha Troops began to flood the streets. There was panic and chaos all around. Alpha Troops captured the pedestrians and forced them into a military transport. The jet black transport waited and watched until the driver noticed two Alpha Troops walking toward them. The vehicle sped away with all the fury it had as it approached the building. As the transport took off, a pair of Alpha Troop men jumped into a military vehicle and gave chase to the transport that sped away. As the Alpha Troopers left the area, a transport identical to the one that had pulled in front of the building, pulled out of a nearby parking garage and gave chase to the Alpha Troops.

The first transport weaved down the city streets but did not dodge civilians like the last time. They weaved between Alpha Troops and their transports. More Alpha Troops tried to stop the vehicle but the transport wasted no time in running down any Alpha Troops who dared to stand in their way. The chase went on and the Alpha Troops tried to force the transport off the road until the second transport caught up to the chase.

The second vehicle pulled alongside the Alpha Troops transport and a window was partially rolled down. From the window, the barrel of a weapon was aimed at the Alpha Troops. The Alpha Troops driver's window was rolled down and the driver tried to aim a pistol at the second transport. The weapon from the transport was fired twice and two darts hit the driver in the head. The Alpha Troop transport swerved and crashed into the façade of a building, sending bricks and a fireball into the air.

The first transport slammed on its brakes and spun around and burned rubber the entire time. It rushed back to the destroyed transport. The second transport disappeared into the confusion still taking place with the Alpha Troops as they gathered the people on the streets. The first transport came to a stop near the crashed vehicle and two females got out, dressed in full Alpha Troops combat gear, although they were nowhere near the size of normal Alpha Troopers.

The two females quickly pulled the passenger of the crashed transport out and pushed a dart into his neck. The Alpha Trooper convulsed as the females stuffed him into the trunk of their transport and quickly sped away from the fire-engulfed transport. As they sped away the Alpha Troops who had been gathering the other people on the streets finished their work. All the troop transport vehicles sped away toward an arena near the industrial district.

The vehicle with an Alpha Trooper in the trunk, rushed back toward the building it had been set in front of just moments earlier. The transport pulled into a parking garage across the street. The second transport was already sitting in the garage. Its occupants had quickly destroyed all the cameras in the garage so no one would be able to see what was about to happen.

The two females got out of their transport and opened the rear hatch. They pulled the Alpha Trooper out of the back and proceeded to hit, kick and punch the Alpha Trooper for a solid minute before one of the females held him up while the other squared up in front of him. The one facing him pulled her helmet off to reveal it was Crystal Dakota.

"You will do what I tell you without question," Dakota barked. "Do you understand?"

"What are you doing to me?" the Alpha Trooper begged. "The pain...what did you do?"

"You will go across the street to the bank," Dakota commanded. "My partner and I will follow you. You will gain access into the bank and find out how many people are currently inside."

"Refuse," the trooper begged in pain.

"September," Dakota said, "release him."

September released her hold on the man and he slowly stood up. Dakota looked at him for a moment before she leveled two massive kicks to the man's head. Dakota moved so quickly he didn't even see the kicks coming until he was on the ground. The Alpha Trooper screamed out in pain and he covered his head as he writhed in pain on the ground. Dakota kicked him again before signaling September to pick him up.

"As I said," Dakota continued, "you will get into the bank and find out how many people are inside. Do you understand?"

"Go to hell," the man said as he spit blood at Dakota's feet.

Dakota smiled before moving blindingly fast. She slit the Trooper's throat from ear to ear. The man grabbed at his neck but it was too late; he was dead before he hit the ground. The doors to the other transport opened up and three people walked out. Two women dressed like Alpha Females and one male dressed like an Alpha Male. They all wore the helmets but took them off as they approached the dead trooper on the ground. Doctor Kent, Jerrica, and Nyx looked over Dakota's handiwork.

"Plan B," Dakota said. "There was no way he would have helped us."

"What's Plan B?" Doctor Kent asked.

"Have your dart guns ready," Dakota said as they took supplies out of the trunk of the transports. "And be ready for a fight."

The group got their guns ready and walked toward the bank. They all had their helmets on. The streets of the city were dead; there were no transports, no people, nothing. The Alpha Troopers had chased everyone away. Doctor Kent wondered how they were going to get through the door but as they got closer he didn't have to wonder very long.

As Dakota got closer to the door she increased her speed so she was almost running when she hit the door. The door shook but didn't break. It did however alert the personnel in the bank something was going on. Dakota grabbed onto the door and struggled with all her might. She slowly ripped the reinforced door off its hinges. The rest of the group had their guns at the ready while the Troopers inside stood dumbfounded at what was happening.

After only a few moments of struggling, the door had been ripped off and all the Alpha Troops in the bank got hit in their unprotected neck skin with darts. Dakota and September fought with the four troops who had been completely covered. The fight was fast paced and the two women were outnumbered and vastly outsized. They still had no trouble quickly taking the Alpha Troops to the ground and pulling their helmets off, which allowed them to be shot with the darts.

When the troops in the entrance lobby had been killed, the group quickly fanned out and scanned the entire area. The first thing they noticed was the bank didn't have a traditionally lobby and teller windows. There was a lobby surrounded by offices. The lobby contained a number of overstuffed chairs and sofas, but there were no banking windows. The group quickly rushed through each office and killed three more Alpha Troops in the process before they found what they had been looking for.

As Dakota entered a main office, large and full of books and papers, she heard a noise in a tall upright cabinet. Dakota had her gun at the ready and opened the cabinet as she pulled out a distinguished looking man in his mid-fifties. Dakota threw the man to the ground and held him at gunpoint. He was a big man, but well put together. He wore a navy three piece suit and had graying hair, wide brown eyes and a large nose. The man trembled as Dakota pulled him off the ground with one hand and pushed him against the wall.

"Who are you?" Dakota barked.

"I...I...I'm...Bank president," the man stuttered. "D...D...Darrel..."

"That's all I need to know Darrel," Dakota shouted pushing the barrel of the gun directly into his mouth. "Here's all you need to know, you are going to open the vault to this bank then go wait in the lobby with one of my friends here. You signal any alarms, you call anyone, you so much as move without permission and you will be instantly shot. Do I make myself clear Darrel?"

Darrel nodded his head as he continued to tremble with fear. Dakota pulled the gun out of his mouth and motioned for him to start moving.

"Take us to the vault," Dakota commanded.

Darrel led the group through the bank lobby to an elevator. He had to use a black key card and code to activate the elevator. When his codes cleared, the doors opened up. Dakota motioned September to stay in the lobby and watch for any activity while the rest of the group loaded onto the elevator. Darrel pushed a button to go to the basement and had to enter another code in order to get the elevator to operate.

When the elevator reached the bottom floor, the doors opened and the group entered into a small, sterile room with nothing in it. There was only the elevator and the vault door. The room was barely big enough for the group to stand in. Darrel was prompted by Dakota's gun to walk over to the vault door and enter the codes. He used two identical key cards and two codes to open the vault door.

The group entered the vault and had been stunned by what they saw. It was a luxurious room, opulent, with fine chairs, rugs, paintings, ornate carpets and statues. To one side was another vault door, but the room looked to have been in a mansion rather than a bank.

"Strange room this is," Doctor Kent said. "What is the meaning of this?"

"This room," Darrel said, "is for when people come to use things from their vaults. Whether they need to look over or sign papers, use something they had in there, whatever, this room is for the people who hold items in the vault."

"Strange," Nyx said. "I thought this bank was for empire use only?"

"It is," Darrel said. "And the empire does a lot of business here, which is why you people will never get away with this. You're going to be in a lot of trouble."

"No we won't," Dakota said. "Open the other vault door."

"I don't have access to that vault," Darrel said.

"The bank president," Dakota said pushing her gun into his chest, "doesn't have access to his own vault? That I don't believe. Remember what I said in your office, you will do as I tell you or you will die. Make a choice. Open the door or I pull the trigger. Before you get any funny ideas, I can open that vault on my own, you saw what I did to the front door. Having you open it would be much simpler and cleaner, but I will shoot you and rip it open if need be."

"I told you," Darrel said. "I don't have…"

Darrel was cut off by the sound of a gun. He looked down to see blood seeping from his body. He felt a strange pain in his chest but it didn't last long. Darrel was dead before the pain registered. Dakota went to the vault door and sized the situation up.

"Do you think you can actually rip that door off?" Nyx asked.

"Maybe," Dakota said. "But I think I might have a better idea."

Dakota ripped the decorations off the wall around the vault door. Once she got to the bare wall, Dakota grabbed a smaller metal statue and used it to rip down the drywall overlay. When a door sized hole had been exposed, Dakota stopped and investigated the wall.

"Just as I thought," Dakota said. "The door is massive and heavy. The lock is surely so secure we will never bypass it. The walls of the vault are simply brick though, maybe steel reinforced, but nothing I can't get through."

Dakota took the statue again and pounded it against the brick wall. The force at which she hit the wall was intense and caused the statue to vibrate with each and every hit. As she continued to hit the wall with great force, the brick gave way. Before long, the statue was destroyed. Dakota grabbed another statue and continued. The bricks kept falling away and the group saw steel beams that ran up and down the wall. Dakota dropped the statue and pulled on the beams. It took all of her strength but she was able to create an opening big enough for the group to squeeze through.

The vault was dark inside. The only light was coming through the hole Dakota had made. The group scrambled to find a light source. Doctor Kent found a panel on the wall that controlled the vault. He turned on the lights and was able to open the door from the inside. When the lights came on the group was stunned at what they saw.

Inside the vault was crate after crate, floor to ceiling, wall to wall, of the amino acid. There were boxes and boxes full of them. The walls of the vault were bare and there was nothing else inside.

"This helps our cause," Jerrica said opening on of the boxes and looking inside. "There must be enough here to supply the state for a year."

"I'd say that's a damn good estimate," Doctor Kent said as he looked at the control panel.

"What makes you say that?" Jerrica asked.

"I'm looking over some of the dates on this screen," Doctor Kent said. "The log of who came and left, how long they stayed, stuff like that. This room is only opened once a year to be emptied and refilled."

"They rotate the supply," Nyx said. "They don't want it to get old."

"There must be other banks like this then," Jerrica said.

"If I had to guess," Doctor Kent said, "I would say one for each of the sixty-four states."

"What's our play then?" Nyx asked. "What do we do with all of this?"

"We take it," Doctor Kent said typing something into his communicator. "I'm calling some of our transports and people here. We will clean this bank out. Dakota, get September and start carrying these crates topside. Nyx, get looking for the information drive. Did they give you some clue on where it could be?"

"It was exact," Nyx said. "I need a boost though,"

Nyx was standing underneath a vent shaft. Doctor Kent moved a couple boxes in place and helped Nyx get on top of them. She opened the lid to the vent and reached inside. Her hand was only there a moment before she pulled it back and held a small, black, pen sized device. Nyx smiled from ear to ear.

"I thought you said it was in a baseboard?" Jerrica asked.

"I didn't know if we could trust everyone in the room when I said that," Nyx said. "The drive was fastened to the top of the vent so even if someone placed their hand inside to look for it on the bottom, they wouldn't have found it."

"Brilliant," Doctor Kent said. "Give it here."

Nyx handed the drive to Doctor Kent who quickly hooked it to his computer.

"I'm going to send this to multiple computers," Doctor Kent said. "All within our group. That way, even if we are caught they can still save people."

"Why don't you just send it to the media?" Jerrica asked. "And the news wires?"

"Why not send it to some international peacekeeping organizations?" Nyx asked.

"Well I'll be damned," Doctor Kent said.

"What is it?" Nyx asked.

"Clever," Doctor Kent said.

"What?" Jerrica asked.

"The amino acid," Doctor Kent said, "is not pure. It never was. It's only a partial to begin with, which is what caused so much confusion, but then, it's also mutated. The Shackle Virus mutated us, changed us. I knew it was powerful but this is amazing. I didn't even know they had the technology to do this back then."

"Is there a way to reverse it?" Jerrica asked.

"Not only is there a way to reverse it," Doctor Kent said, "but there's enough compound right here in Two Rivers. They are storing it at the facility where they manufacture the amino acid. We'll have to work quickly, but we must storm the plant and take it. There will be enough there to reverse the effects for about half of the population. We can work quickly and within a month or two have the rest of the population safe."

Jerrica was about to ask another question when workers entered the vault to take the amino acid out. There were only a few workers, but along with Dakota and September they wasted no time getting the crates topside and loaded onto transports. Doctor Kent led Nyx and Jerrica back to the main lobby of the bank.

There were two transport vehicles backed up to the bank doors with many guards rushing about. The crates of the amino acid were being carefully stacked into the transports. It didn't take the crew long to have everything stacked, secured, and the transport doors closed.

The transports took off while Doctor Kent, Jerrica, Nyx, Dakota, and September walked toward their transports in the garage across the street. As they walked, shots rang out from above. In the blink of an eye, Doctor Kent, Jerrica, and Nyx were on the ground in a dull pain that quickly subsided before they blacked out. Dakota and September got into defensive positions as Alpha Troops rushed into the street.

There were ten troops in all, mainly men who surrounded the Beta Troops. Dakota and September wasted no time in attacking the troops. Dakota had two on the ground before they even realized the girls had attacked. The surprise attack didn't last long though, as three men and a woman finally subdued Dakota while two men took September. The attackers pricked both Dakota's and September's necks with needles.

As they pinned the girls to the ground and locked them in shackles and chains, a troop transport truck and a medical transport rushed to the scene. Dakota helplessly watched as Nyx was loaded into the medical transport and the others had been loaded into the military transport. Dakota felt the gurney she'd been placed on lift and start to move. Her mind was a fog and her muscles wouldn't respond. She didn't know what they'd injected her with, only that she was defenseless against it. Orders were shouted out as an Alpha Woman walked up to Dakota. The Alpha swung her arm and a crack was heard against Dakota's skull, everything went black.

Chapter #18

Alexis paced about in a simple rambler house, set in a middle-class district of Two Rivers. The house was far less opulent than she was used to, yet somehow felt more like a home. , Alexis worried she'd never hear word of how much progress her friends had made. Alexis had snuck into the city with Nyx and the other rebels, but split off from them right away. Alexis had her loyal troops and military ready to strike for her and what she believed in.

Alexis wished she could have been with Nyx and the others. She wished she could have seen the Beta Troops in action as they took out the Alpha Troops. She'd given her troops the dart guns with the ability to stop the Alpha Troops. She explained to her troops how to use them. Alexis knew very soon they would turn the quiet neighborhood into the first battle ground of the war and the war would bring about an end to her father's empire.

As Alexis paced back and forth as she waited for any news at all. She removed her long, sleeveless duster and placed it on a chair. She caught a glimpse of her reflection as she looked out a window. Alexis realized she'd developed into a beautiful young woman, even if she hadn't fully grown yet. She looked over her outfit in the reflection at her yellow crop top and navy tights, the same style outfit she'd worn for years. It was the outfit of those who believed like she did.

Alexis picked up her jacket and put it back on as a commander entered the room. The man was wearing a black, one-piece jumpsuit made of smart materials. He carried a large assault rifle in his hands and had two pistols on his belt. He was a big man with a flat face and square jaw. He had a black beard which matched his black hair. The man carried himself with an extremely ridged posture. He had been one of Alexis's top commanders since she started leading troops. She trusted him more than any of her military troops.

"Commander Paulson," Alexis said as he saluted her and she saluted back, "do you bring a report?"

"I do Alexis," Commander Paulson said in a deep voice. "We've just received word the heist at the bank went almost as planned."

"Almost?"

"The bank had been storing the amino acid," Commander Paulson said quickly. "A massive store of it. Doctor Kent ordered transports in and they removed the cargo. The rebels have a large supply of the amino acid."

"That's a good thing," Alexis said. "If my father tries to destroy supplies of it as revenge for losing his empire we can at least keep some people alive. There's more to this report though?"

"There is my lady," Commander Paulson said. "They retrieved the drive but when attempting to exit the building, the entire group was captured."

"Captured?" Alexis asked as she fell into a chair from going weak in the knees. "Nyx?"

"Nyx was loaded into a medical transport," Commander Paulson said. "The others were taken in a military transport. Both vehicles were heavily guarded with Alpha Troops."

"I had your men and women," Alexis said standing again, "guarding my friends. They were of the utmost importance. You'd better have a damn good explanation as to how they were able to be captured. You know the instant Charlie finds out Nyx really isn't pregnant he will strangle her himself."

"Be calm my lady," Commander Paulson said. "We have people on them and they will not make it to their destinations.

We must be careful though, we don't want to kill them while trying to get them back."

"They'd better return to me unharmed," Alexis said.

"They will," Commander Paulson replied.

"And the drive?" Alexis asked. "They found it? Were they able to get anything from it before they were captured? We they able to keep it out of my father's hands?"

"I wouldn't worry about that my lady," Commander Paulson said.

"I'd better not have to," Alexis said. "What can we do to help them here Commander Paulson? What should our course of action be?"

"We should extract them from the transports soon," Commander Paulson said. "But the second we do, every Alpha Troop will be after us. There will be no easy way to do it without giving ourselves away."

"Then that's exactly what we'll do," Alexis said. "We have troops in position, Commander Paulson. Doctor Kent has turned the command of some of his troops to me as well. Send out orders to attack the amino acid plant and at the same time start riots here in this residential area."

"My lady?" Commander Paulson asked.

"It will cause confusion," Alexis said. "The empire will be forced to send troops, troops that he now can't send to follow our friends as we rescue them."

"Good thinking," Commander Paulson said.

"Send the orders now Commander Paulson," Alexis said. "Tell the troops here to start a riot in the streets. There must be mass confusion and terror. We've taken all the people out of their homes so no civilians will die. There'll be damage, but it can and will be repaired. Have snipers in position to take out the Alpha Troops when they arrive."

"It will be done my lady," Commander Paulson said as he took out a communicator.

Alexis watched from the window and didn't have to wait long before troops poured out of the houses and damaged the property. They fired guns in the air and burned down houses. Alexis knew it wouldn't take long before Alpha Troops would be dispatched to the area to quell the violence.

Alexis took another look at the mayhem occurring outside the house and went to a rudimentary command post she had setup in the house. She looked over the viewer and brought up screens which showed the amino acid factory. Alexis could see the four-block area. She was on the edge of where the immediate violence was occurring.

Alexis got the video viewers up to show the factory. All looked calm until Alpha Troops started falling over, followed up by getting hit with sniper rifles. The Alpha Troops still standing were in a state of panicked confusion. No one seemed to know what was going on. There were more shots followed by more Alpha Troops falling over.

In a flash, all the view screens went white. It took a moment for the cameras to refocus themselves. Alexis saw a bomb had detonated on the wall surrounding the factory. There was a massive, ten foot hole in the wall. It was big enough for troop transports to enter the compound. She smiled as she saw a massive troop transport racing into the main area of the factory.

Rebel troops poured out of the back of the transport and shot in all directions. The Alpha Troops fell at a fast rate. They weren't able to combat the tainted darts hitting them in the exposed parts of their necks. Bullets flew in all directions.

Alexis saw a group had reached the doors but couldn't open them. They placed a package near the drive-through door and all the troops ran and ducked for cover. It only took a moment before another blast rocked the area and a gaping hole was in the side of the factory.

Alexis's eyes had been glued to the viewer when Commander Paulson rushed back into the room.

"My lady," Commander Paulson said. "We must get you out of here."

"No commander," Alexis said. "I want to watch close up what happens to my troops. I will stay with them."

"I cannot allow that," Commander Paulson said sternly. "There are reports of massive amounts of Alpha Troops heading in this direction. We cannot risk you getting captured, not at this juncture. You must come with me."

"Where will we go?" Alexis asked mockingly. "Where? All the exits of this city are blocked off."

"We must get you in a safer house than this," Commander Paulson said. "I insist my lady. You must come with me now."

"You still didn't tell me where you want to take me," Alexis said.

Alexis turned her back to the Commander so he wouldn't see the tear that fell down her cheek. Alexis had always loved the commander and the work he did. She couldn't believe he was a traitor to her, but his actions called his loyalty into question. Alexis pulled a knife with a six inch blade from her jacket. She placed the knife in the front of her tights as she slipped off her jacket and allowed it to fall to the floor.

Alexis kept her back toward Commander Paulson while she silently un-sheaved the knife. She held the knife tight against her stomach while Commander Paulson slowly inched toward her.

"You must go now," Commander Paulson insisted again.

"Tell me where you will take me?" Alexis asked.

"I'll take you," Commander Paulson said as he roughly grabbed Alexis around the waist with both hands, "straight to your father where you belong. Maybe he will teach you some…"

Commander Paulson was cut off in mid-sentence as Alexis first drove the knife into his right wrist. As he tried to process the surprise attack, she spun around and buried the knife into his throat. Commander Paulson coughed once before collapsed to the floor in a pool of blood. Alexis pull the knife out of the commander and wiped the blade on his clothing. She quickly began a search of his person, taking his guns, knives, and communicators.

In his breast pocket Alexis discovered a scrap of paper. It was a note which was written from her father to the Commander. The only thing it said was Alexis must be brought before him. She must be bound, drugged and in no way able to make a counter attack. The revelation that her father wanted to see her before he killed her startled her, but she reasoned he must have wanted to ask about the structure of her resistance and how he could be sure it was all destroyed before she died.

Alexis quickly looked out of the house again and saw Alpha Troops had entered the area. She couldn't be sure how many her father would send but she felt confident her troops would defeat them. The thought dawned on Alexis that if Commander Paulson worked with her father, others could have been as well. She wondered at who else would be against her but would smile and salute her as she walked by.

Alexis looked back at the viewer and saw her troops had the factory under lockdown. There were piles of Alpha Troop bodies being burned. Her men used transports to take the amino acid from the factory. Alexis smiled as she watched and knew the first wave of the campaign was going well. She could have done without a traitor, but Alexis knew things like that were bound to come up.

As Alexis watched the mayhem, the door to the house flew open and a female troop rushed in. She was dressed in a black one-piece body suit like the Alpha Women wore but she didn't have a helmet on. Alexis immediately pulled a gun on the woman who dropped her pistol and placed her hands in the air.

"I have a report for you my lady," the trooper said.

"Go on," Alexis said, still holding the gun on the woman.

"We've engaged with many Alpha Troops in the streets here and defeated most of them. Your father didn't send near as many as we expected. There seems to be rioting in many parts of the city, not just here. We're not sure yet what set things off. Your father has taken a group of hostages into his compound and with the troops he has left, he's fortifying the outer walls, so we cannot risk a frontal assault."

"Has there been any word from the group who hit the bank?" Alexis asked as she lowered the gun. "Have they been saved yet?"

"Saved?" the woman asked. "I haven't heard anything."

"How many troops were sent to extract them?"

"My lady?"

"How many troops?" Alexis almost screamed. "Paulson said a team was going to extract them."

"I saw all the orders that Commander Paulson gave," the woman said. "And he never said anything about extracting the group who hit the bank."

In that moment, it dawned on Alexis that Commander Paulson was loyal to her father, never to her. Her friends had been on their way to the castle compound and there was no way for her to save them. They would be almost to the castle at that point. Alexis knew that there was only one thing left to do.

"Get as many troops together as you can," Alexis said. "We are storming the castle."

Chapter #19

Emperor Ross II, Prime Minister Garret Boyd and multiple Alpha Troops stood on a platform in the decorated courtyard of the palace. In front of them were hundreds of news cameras with reporters and media everywhere. Every reporter in Two Rivers had been rounded up and brought to the castle when the city was sealed off. Emperor Ross II smiled, knowing what he was about to do. He knew for certain it would be the end of the problems they'd been having with the empire.

As he watched, a group of hostages had been brought into the courtyard by Alpha Troops. The media filmed the entire process. The people looked to be sick and ready to die. Charlie and Garret had captured those people when they first got to the City of Falling Stars and had held them for almost a week.

From another doorway, Alpha Troops brought in Doctor Kent, Doctor Prowl, and Jerrica. Charlie had hoped to have Monty meet with Jerrica before the event took place but there simply wasn't time. Once the group had been taken from the bank, Charlie knew they had to move. He had received reports about riots taking place in the country. He had no clue why. Charlie wanted the people to be afraid and suffer, and he knew his plan would be the way. Once everyone was in place, Charlie moved to a podium with a cluster of microphones.

"Greetings U-Cam," Charlie said in a regal tone. "It pains me to say, but our country is in danger. There are so many people who only want chaos and terror. It's my job to protect you, all of you, from the pains of these evil, mad people. It's my deepest regret things have gotten this out of control. I wanted to be peaceful but these monsters will not allow it. These people, right here," Charlie motioned to the trio in cuffs surrounded by Alpha Troops, "have robbed government banks. They attempted to steal and destroy spare supplies of the amino acids. These rebels want people in this country to die. I will not allow this kind of madness to continue. We have sealed off the great city of Two Rivers and the City of Falling Stars and have done so in order to capture all the rebels. We know there are many more rebels in this city and we want them to turn themselves over to us immediately so no more people have to suffer and die. With us today are people who are suffering because of these rebels. I have asked a special young man to come up and plead for all the people in this city, and this country who want peace and prosperity and for all those people who want the empire. This young man will beg the rebels to turn themselves in as the price for these people's lives. The rebels must be stopped and this is the only way. Billy Hedge, please step forward."

From the crowd of people, a young boy not older than ten years old stepped forward. He was dusty and dirty and wore tattered clothing. He had a mop of black hair in need of a trim and his eyes were so sad they would have broken anyone's heart. Billy slowly made his way to the stage and up to Emperor Ross II. The emperor handed Billy a microphone. Everyone in the crowd went silent as Billy took a deep breath and began to speak.

"We've been under lock for almost a week," Billy said slowly. "I don't know what happened in the country or why we were placed under lock. There's so much I don't understand about this country and government but I agree with Emperor Ross II that something must be done." Billy paused for a moment to look at Charlie and Garret before he took a deep breath and continued. "But I don't agree with them on how to do it. Emperor Ross II and his Prime Minister Garret Boyd are monsters. They are the ones destroying the country. I speak for all the people you have arrested here and we say go ahead and kill us. We will not beg anyone to turn themselves in. We are cheering the rebels on and hope they take this country over."

The people in the crowd cheered and yelled profanities at the emperor. They threw rocks, trash, anything they could get their hands on at the Alpha Troops. The media recorded all of it as Emperor Ross II ordered the Alpha Troops to turn their guns on the prisoners and open fire. The Alpha Troops were on the verge of opening fire when gunfire filled the air.

The emperor looked out past the castle wall and saw hundreds of troops and people moving toward the castle. Troops threw grenades at the wall and quickly brought it down, which allowed the troops to rush in. Charlie ordered the Alpha Troops to engage but before they could, a cascade of expertly shot darts flew into the courtyard and hit the Alpha Troops in exposed skin areas. It caused over half the Alpha Troops to fall to the ground. Charlie was stunned at the sight.

"Those are Alexis's troops," Garret shouted over the noise of battle as the remaining Alpha Troops opened fire. "We have to get inside."

"Let those people die," Charlie yelled as he grabbed an Alpha Trooper. "Kill all the people out there. Every last one of them."

"Sir," the troop said. "Yes sir."

"Take those three and follow me," Charlie yelled to another trooper as the first one killed Billy.

Charlie rushed into the castle and Garret followed. Two Alpha Troops herded the trio into the castle. Charlie rushed down the halls and around the corners. He wanted to get to his command room as quickly as he could. Before they went to the platform he'd heard an attack had happened on the factory that manufactured the amino acid but there hadn't been a report since. When he reached the door he stopped and addressed the pair of Alpha Troops with him.

"Take these three and lock them up," Charlie barked. "I will deal with them momentarily."

The Alpha Troops took the trio and rushed down the hall as Charlie and Garret entered the room. Inside the room was a mad house. People rushed everywhere as video viewers played the news. There was panic in the air. Even the pair of female Alpha Troops guarding the door seemed to be nervous. Charlie saw the panic on people's faces and couldn't figure out what their problem was.

"There's no need to worry people," Charlie yelled. "Alexis's troops will be defeated. There's no way they can get into the castle. We'll be safe here."

"It's not that sir," a woman at a network machine said turning in her chair. "There are problems much bigger than that."

"What?" Charlie barked. "What's going on?"

"There was a report over the network," the woman said. "The media picked it up, as did other countries. The report is running constantly."

"What is it?" Garret demanded.

"The formula for the amino acid," the woman said meekly. "Along with a way to permanently reverse the effects."

"They found the information drive," Charlie said as he fell stunned into a chair. "What do we do?"

"This isn't good Charlie," Garret said. "We don't have many options left."

"What can we do?" Charlie asked. "If they know the formula, know how to reverse it, what cards do we hold? Alpha Troops? I'm sure once we hit everyone with Alpha Troops they'll release the formula to take them out too. Is there anything we can do?"

"I don't know," Garret said. "We need to think."

"No," Charlie said standing. "We need to act. Follow me."

Charlie rushed out of the room with Garret two steps behind him. They raced down the hallways and into the holding cell area. In one cell, Doctor Prowl, Doctor Kent and Jerrica were locked in chains. In the opposite cell, Dakota and September had been chained up against a wall. Charlie stood outside the cells and looked at the prisoners.

"You think you've defeated me?" Charlie said. "You think you've brought down the empire?"

"You can have your information drive back," Doctor Kent said with a smile. "We really don't need it anymore."

"Arrogant fool," Charlie yelled. "You really think this will be the end of the empire? I wanted you all here to witness the final plan. Once this is executed you will know what real fear is. This will be the final attempt to take the empire down."

"What do you plan to do?" Jerrica asked.

"The Beta Troops," Charlie said. "No one knows how many we really have. Hundreds of them."

Charlie opened the door to Dakota and September's cell. He entered and walked right up to Dakota. She was chained up and still foggy from the compound they'd hit her with. Charlie slapped her before kissing her. He laughed as she tried to resist but couldn't. Charlie took her chains off, causing Dakota to fall to the floor. He laughed again.

"Look how pathetic you are," Charlie said. "So weak you cannot even defend yourself. Should I kill you first or your partner?"

"How?" Dakota struggled to say.

"How did I do this?" Charlie smugly said. "Simple. We created a compound to weaken Beta Troops so we could put you on the ground and stop you until given the antidote. We never had this for Alpha Troops but I realized it was more than necessary. I will release the Alpha Troops and have them fight your rebels. Once you think you've destroyed all of them, I will release the Beta Troops. You will have no clue who they are or where they are coming from. They will be unstoppable. These two are nothing compared to some of the Beta Troops we have in training. They are genetically perfect. We've engineered them to be perfect. Totally loyal, strong, smart, and perfect."

"You'll never have enough to win," Doctor Kent said. "We have too many troops."

"Really?" Charlie asked. "There's a little secret about the Beta Troops you don't know. Their age."

"Age?" Jerrica asked.

"Dakota here," Charlie said. "She is only about two years old. Growth acceleration in the engineering chambers. We have thousands of these troops. All we have to do is go to the factories they were made and wake them up."

"Impossible," Dakota said still trying to stand. "I remember my childhood, growing up."

"Memory implants," Charlie said. "Very easy to implement in the chambers. It had to be done though. The new troops we have ready to go have implants telling them how horrible they were treated by the rebels. They have memories of living in a city where they were tormented by the rebels, where the rebels beat them, stole from them and killed one or both of their parents. They all believe they signed up to work for me. They all believe their lives were destroyed by the rebels."

Charlie pulled a gun out of his jacket and walked to the door of the other cell. He raised his gun, pulled the trigger and shot Doctor Prowl between the eyes. Jerrica screamed out and cried as her older brother fell limp in his chains.

"Why did you do that?" Jerrica screamed.

"Because he was playing both sides," Charlie said.

"Kill me," Jerrica said.

"Never," Charlie said putting the gun away. "You will be put back in the pleasure houses. You will be the best little whore out there, all thanks to your big brother."

"You monster," Jerrica said through her tears.

"Empires take sacrifice," Charlie said walking back to the other cell. "And you are the ones who need to do the sacrificing. All you had to do was follow my orders and live the life we laid out for you. But no, you had to lead this little rebellion, which is now over."

Charlie walked up to Dakota who had been standing but bracing herself against the wall. He slapped her again as he sadistically smiled. Dakota had a hard time standing. Charlie loved every moment of it. He did not even care about what was going on elsewhere in the empire.

"I've learned so much about the Beta Troops from you Dakota," Charlie said. "You have no idea how much you've helped me. The information we got from watching you will be proven valuable as the new wave of Beta Troops are unleashed over the empire."

"There's one thing you're forgetting about the Beta Troops," Dakota said weakly. "Something I never had time to tell you about."

"What's that?" Charlie asked.

Dakota's hand shot out and slammed into Charlie's chest. She punched Charlie multiple times in the heart, so rapidly the others barely saw her hands move. Dakota stopped and stood powerfully as Charlie fell to the ground.

"Beta Troops," Dakota said as she slammed her fist into Charlie's heart one more time. "Are amazing actors and your compound really doesn't work."

One more punch and Charlie was dead on the floor. Garret tried to run but Dakota was much too fast for him. She caught him and twisted his neck, killing him instantly. September broke her chains and assisted Dakota in getting the others out of their chains. Jerrica looked at her brother but realized there was nothing they could do to get him back at this point.

"He was a good man," Doctor Kent said. "He only wanted to protect you."

"I know," Jerrica said. "Mom and dad would have been proud. He was a good brother."

"We need to find Alexis," Doctor Kent said. "She needs to assume the empire."

"I know where Nyx is being held," Dakota said. "I can guess anyway. Follow me."

The group rushed through the castle and very quickly entered the hospital area. Just as Dakota had predicted, Nyx had been strapped down to a hospital table and prepped for an examination.

"Did they do anything to you?" Doctor Kent asked.

"No," Nyx said. "No doctors ever came here. I haven't seen anyone since they brought me here."

"Good," Doctor Kent said as he held her down and undid the straps. "Where will we find Alexis?"

"Is Charlie dead?" Nyx asked getting up.

"Charlie, Garret, and my brother," Jerrica said.

"I'm so sorry," Nyx said. "We still have work to do though. Alexis told me she would take the main office of this castle. In the ancient past it would have been called the throne room. That's where we will meet her."

"Let's move," Dakota said.

The group rushed out of the room. There was fighting going on in some of the hallways. Dead Alpha Troops lined the floors of the hallways. The rebels were sparing none of the empires genetic killers. When the group arrived in the throne room, Alexis and her personal security had been there waiting. Alexis rushed to Nyx and hugged her.

"You made it," Alexis said. "Where is my father?"

"Dead," Dakota said. "I killed him along with the Prime Minister."

"Good," Alexis said. "His empire of evil has ended. I declare myself, Alexis Ross, the new emperor. My first decree is that Nyx is the new Prime Minister. My second decree is that elections for representatives will be held as soon as possible."

"Those are some very good decrees," Doctor Kent said. "There's much work that needs to be done though."

"I have a question I'm afraid to ask," Dakota said. "Charlie had created hundreds of Beta Troops and stored them in genetic engineering tanks."

"Yes," Alexis said. "I am aware. They can be awakened as soon as two years after the process was started."

"What are you going to do with them?" Dakota asked.

"We have to destroy them," Alexis said. "They are far too powerful to leave alive, especially if they were to fall into the wrong hands. All the Alpha Troops will be destroyed in this war."

"What about us?" Dakota asked. "Do you wish us to destroy ourselves right now?"

"Not exactly yet," Alexis said with a smile. "You are loyal to me now and will serve as my personal security, does that sound acceptable?"

"It does," Dakota said. "Thank you."

"There will be a place for all of you," Alexis said. "Doctor Kent, every troop you had will have a place in the empire. You two will be advisors to the government."

"Advisors?" Doctor Kent asked.

"To keep us on track," Alexis said. "To make sure we stay on the right path."

"I like that," Jerrica said.

"There's much work to do," Alexis said. "And not much time to do it in. We must bring this country back to what it was. That is my pledge and I want all of you to hold me to it. Follow me to help quell the people and stop the violence. Today is a new day."

It didn't take long for Alexis and her troops to wipe all the Alpha Troops from U-Cam. Alexis kept her word and held elections for a president and representatives. Alexis won the presidential election and kept her word to all the people. The governments were from then on for the people, by the people, and are there to serve the people.

About Leif J. Erickson

Leif Erickson was born and raised on a grain farm outside Wheaton, MN, just a stone's throw from White Rock, SD, which served as the inspiration for the Ghost Town series. From a very early age, Leif knew that he was going to be a farmer, just like his father and grandfather. As he grew up, Leif learned everything he could about farming, always riding in equipment with his dad and helping out wherever he could.

After Leif graduated high school he attended North Dakota State University in Fargo, North Dakota, where he achieved a BS in Agricultural Economics along with a minor in History. During his time in college, Leif networked with many other farmers from across North Dakota, South Dakota, and Minnesota, while advancing his knowledge in all aspects of agricultural. With a diploma in hand, Leif returned to the family farm and started his career as a farmer.

The first season was very successful and stood as a testament to the hard work and education that Leif had received. All signs pointed to a lifetime career as a farmer until a family tragedy struck and the family farm was dispersed. For the first time in his life, Leif didn't know what he wanted to pursue for a career.

Leif returned to Fargo, ND where he began his career as a stock and futures trader. It was during this time that he began to become serious about writing. With one computer watching the markets, Leif would be on the other, writing. Leif quickly realized though that Fargo wasn't the city or location that he wanted to make a home in. Less than one year since he moved there, Leif moved to Plymouth MN, in the Twins Cities area.

Continuing with the trading and writing, Leif began to learn everything that he could about writing, about storytelling, and about the hero's journey. Leif spent his spare time reading novels or books about writing. It was during his time in the Cities that Leif wrote many, many different stories, getting the outlines and first drafts finished. In the three years that Leif was in the Cities, he wrote the first draft for over fifty different stories.

Leif received information about a career opportunity that was back in his hometown of Wheaton so he returned to go to work for the local grain elevator. The work was hard and the days were long without much time for writing. Leif missed being able to write every day. He had so many more stories that he wanted to write. Being aggressive and a hard worker, Leif quickly moved up the ladder in the company and within six months he was in a management position.

Although Leif had met and dated many women when he was in the Twin Cities, it was in Wheaton where he met the new Science Teacher at his old High School and within fifteen months of meeting the pair were married at Good Shepherd Lutheran Church in Wheaton. Many have described the pair as absolutely made for each other, and they spend much of their time hiking in State Parks or canoeing the local lakes and rivers.

Being back in Wheaton, Leif used his free time to polish up and finish some of his stories. He got two stories to the point where he was satisfied to bring them to the marketplace and share them with others. Although he still works for the elevator, Leif looks forward to the day when he can write fulltime, offering more novels and screenplays to entertain and delight others.

Throughout his life, Leif was always quick to be able to tell a story. He had an uncanny ability to quickly make up a story on the spot (sometimes to the dismay of parents and teachers) and to pull people into the story with wild characters, amazing locations, and fantastical storylines. Although Leif focuses on science fiction, he's written stories in many different genera's including mystery, horror, teen comedy, western, and even a little romance.

Throughout Leif's writings you can see traces of his farm life and his love of nature. Being an ecologist and former farmer, much of Leif's writings feature forests, lakes, and nature in general. Leif has always been interested in science and what's possible for the human race, pushing the envelope of technologies, and finding how far humans can go. Much of Leif's science fiction writing explores these themes and ideas.

When he's not writing, Leif and his wife Brittany can be found working on their goal of hiking in every State Park in Minnesota or on the lakes and rivers in a canoe. The pair have some big canoe adventures planned, and have already canoed, from end to end, big lakes such as Lake Traverse and Big Stone Lake. Every once in a while, Leif will pull out his old Disc Jockey system and play a dance as the 'Leif of the Party DJ Service.'

Leif has been influenced by many different writers and stories. His all-time favorite story is 'Sleepy Hollow' by Washington Irving, a story that Leif reads every Halloween. Other influences on his work are the 'Dune' series by Frank Herbert, 'The Lord of the Rings' by J.R.R. Tolkien, and anything related to the Arthurian Legend. Leif also enjoys many other authors such as Charles Dickens, Michael Crichton, John Steinbeck, Isaac Asimov, Neil Gaiman, and F. Scott Fitzgerald just to name a few.

Thank you for checking out a book by Leif Erickson. Please visit his website at www.leifericksonwriting.com and purchase the other books that Leif has written. They will take you on a journey that you will never forget...

www.ingramcontent.com/pod-product-compliance
Lightning Source LLC
Chambersburg PA
CBHW061214170626
46809CB00003B/1356

* 9 7 8 0 9 9 0 7 0 2 5 1 1 *